THE ASIMOV CHRONICLES

FIFTY YEARS OF ISAAC ASIMOV!

V O L U M E F I V E

EDITED BY MARTIN H. GREENBERG

ACE BOOKS, NEW YORK

The stories in this collection are taken from an omnibus edition published in hardcover by Dark Harvest in 1989, titled *The Asimov Chronicles: Fifty Years of Isaac Asimov*.

This collection is a work of fiction. Names, characters, places and incidents are either the product of the author's imagination or are used fictitiously. Any resemblance to actual events or locales, or persons, living or dead, is entirely coincidental.

THE ASIMOV CHRONICLES
VOLUME FIVE

An Ace Book / published by arrangement with
Dark Harvest

PRINTING HISTORY
Dark Harvest edition published 1989
Ace edition / April 1991

ISBN: 0-441-03111-0

Ace Books are published by The Berkley Publishing Group,
200 Madison Avenue, New York, New York 10016.
The name "ACE" and the "A" logo
are trademarks belonging to Charter Communications, Inc.

PRINTED IN THE UNITED STATES OF AMERICA

10 9 8 7 6 5 4 3 2 1

CONTENTS

EXILE TO HELL

"The Russians," said Dowling, in his precise voice, "used to send prisoners to Siberia in the days before space travel had become common. The French used Devil's Island for the purpose. The British sailed them off to Australia."

He considered the chessboard carefully and his hand hesitated briefly over the bishop.

Parkinson, at the other side of the chess board, watched the pattern of the pieces absently. Chess was, of course, the professional game of computer programmers, but, under the circumstances, he lacked enthusiasm. By rights, he felt with some annoyance, Dowling should have been even worse off; he was programming the prosecution's case.

There was, of course, a tendency for the programmer to take over some of the imagined characteristics of the computer—the unemotionality, the imperviousness to anything but logic. Dowling reflected that in his precise hair-part and in the restrained elegance of his clothing.

Parkinson, who preferred to program the defense in the law cases in which he was involved, also preferred to be deliberately careless in the minor aspects of his costume.

He said, "You mean exile is a well-established punishment and therefore not particularly cruel."

"No, it *is* particularly cruel, but also it *is* well-established, and nowadays it has become the perfect deterrent."

Dowling moved the bishop and did not look upward. Parkinson, quite involuntarily, did.

Of course, he couldn't see anything. They were indoors, in the comfortable modern world tailored to human needs, carefully protected against the raw environment. Out there, the night would be bright with its illumination.

When had he last seen it? Not for a long time. It occurred to him to wonder what phase it was in right now. Full? Gleaming? Or was it in its crescent phase? Was it a bright fingernail of light low in the sky?

By rights it should be a lovely sight. Once it had been. But that had been centuries ago, before space travel had become common and cheap, and before the surroundings all about them had grown sophisticated and controlled. Now the lovely light in the sky had become a new and more horrible Devil's Island hung in space.

—No one even used its name any longer, out of sheer distaste. It was "It." Or it was less than that, just a silent, upward movement of the head.

Parkinson said, "You might have allowed me to program the case against exile generally."

"Why? It couldn't have affected the result."

"Not this one, Dowling. But it might have affected future cases. Future punishments might be commuted to the death sentence."

"For someone guilty of equipment damage? You're dreaming."

"It was an act of blind anger. There was intent to harm a human being, granted; but there was no intent to harm equipment."

"Nothing; it means nothing. Lack of intent is no excuse in such cases. You know that."

"It *should* be an excuse. That's my point; the one I wanted to make."

Parkinson advanced a pawn now, to cover his knight.

Dowling considered. "You're trying to hang on to the queen's attack, Parkinson, and I'm not going to let you.—Let's see, now." And while he pondered he said, "These are not primitive times, Parkinson. We live in a crowded world with no margin for error. As small a thing as a blown-out consistor could endanger a sizable fraction of our population. When anger endangers and subverts a power line, it's a serious thing."

"I don't question that—"

"You seemed to be doing so, when you were constructing the defense program."

"I was not. Look, when Jenkins' laser beam cut through the Field-warp, I myself was as close to death as anyone. A quarter hour's additional delay would have meant my end, too, and I'm completely aware of that. My point is only that exile is not the proper punishment!"

He tapped his finger on the chessboard for emphasis, and Dowling caught the queen before it went over. "Adjusting, not moving," he mumbled.

Dowling's eyes went from piece to piece and he continued to hesitate. "You're wrong, Parkinson. It *is* the proper punishment, because there's nothing worse and that matches a crime than which there is nothing worse. Look, we all feel our absolute dependence on a complicated and rather fragile technology. A breakdown might kill us all, and it doesn't matter whether the breakdown is deliberate, accidental, or caused by incompetence. Human beings demand the maximum punishment for any such deed as the only way they can feel secure. Mere death is not sufficient deterrent."

"Yes, it is. No one wants to die."

"They want to live in exile up there even less. That's why we've only had one such case in the last ten years, and only one exile.—There, do something about that!" And Dowling nudged his queen's rook one space to the right.

A light flashed. Parkinson was on his feet at once. "The programming is finished. The computer will have its verdict now."

Dowling looked up phlegmatically, "You've no doubt about what that verdict will be, have you?—Keep the board standing. We'll finish afterward."

Parkinson was quite certain he would lack the heart to continue the game. He hurried down the corridor to the courtroom, light and quick on his feet, as always.

Shortly after he and Dowling had entered, the judge took his seat, and then in came Jenkins, flanked by two guards.

Jenkins looked haggard, but stoical. Ever since the blind rage had overcome him and he had accidentally thrown a sector into unpowered darkness while striking out at a fellow worker, he must have known the inevitable consequence of this worst of all crimes. It helps to have no illusions.

Parkinson was not stoical. He dared not look squarely at Jenkins. He could not have done so without wondering, painfully, as to what might be going through Jenkins' mind at that moment. Was he absorbing, through every sense, all the perfections of familiar comfort before being thrust forever into the luminous Hell that rode the night sky?

Was he savoring the clean and pleasant air in his nostrils, the soft lights, the equable temperature, the pure water on call, the secure surroundings designed to cradle humanity in tame comfort?

While up there—

The judge pressed a contact and the computer's decision was converted into the warm, unmannered sound of a standardized human voice.

"A weighing of all pertinent information in the light of the law of the land and of all relevant precedents leads to the conclusion that Anthony Jenkins is guilty on all counts of the crime of equipment damage and is subject to the maximum penalty."

There were only six people in the courtroom itself, but the entire population was listening by television, of course.

The judge spoke in prescribed phraseology. "The defendant will be taken from here to the nearest spaceport and, on the first available transportation, be removed from this world and sent into exile for the term of his natural life."

Jenkins seemed to shrink within himself, but he said no word.

Parkinson shivered. How many, he wondered, would now feel the enormity of such a punishment for *any* crime? How long before there would be enough humanity among men to wipe out forever the punishment of exile?

Could anyone really think of Jenkins up there in space, without flinching? Could they think, and endure the thought, of a fellow man thrown for all his life among the strange, unfriendly, vicious population of a world of unbearable heat by day and frigid cold by night; of a world where the sky was a harsh blue and the ground a harsher, clashing green; where the dusty air moved raucously and the viscous sea heaved eternally?

And the gravity, that heavy—heavy—heavy—eternal—pull!

Who could bear the horror of condemning someone, for whatever reason, to leave the friendly home of the Moon for that Hell in the sky—the Earth?

FEMININE INTUITION

The Three Laws of Robotics:

1. *A robot may not injure a human being or, through inaction, allow a human being to come to harm.*
2. *A robot must obey the orders given it by human beings except where such orders would conflict with the First Law.*
3. *A robot must protect its own existence as long as such protection does not conflict with the First or Second Law.*

For the first time in the history of United States Robots and Mechanical Men, Inc., a robot had been destroyed through accident on Earth itself.

No one was to blame. The air vehicle had been demolished in mid-air and an unbelieving investigating committee was wondering whether they really dared announce the evidence that it had been hit by a meteorite. Nothing else could have been fast enough to prevent automatic avoidance; nothing else could have done the damage short of a nuclear blast and that was out of the question.

Tie that in with a report of a flash in the night sky just before the vehicle had exploded—and from Flagstaff Observatory, not from an amateur—and the location of a sizable and distinctly meteoric bit of iron freshly gouged into the ground a mile from the site and what other conclusion could be arrived at?

Still, nothing like that had ever happened before and calculations of the odds against it yielded monstrous figures. Yet even colossal improbabilities can happen sometimes.

At the offices of United States Robots, the hows and

whys of it were secondary. The real point was that a robot had been destroyed.

That, in itself, was distressing.

The fact that JN-5 had been a prototype, the first, after four earlier attempts, to have been placed in the field, was even more distressing.

The fact that JN-5 was a radically new type of robot, quite different from anything ever built before, was abysmally distressing.

The fact that JN-5 had apparently accomplished something before its destruction that was incalculably important and that that accomplishment might now be forever gone, placed the distress utterly beyond words.

It seemed scarcely worth mentioning that, along with the robot, the Chief Robo-psychologist of United States Robots had also died.

Clinton Madarian had joined the firm ten years before. For five of those years, he had worked uncomplainingly under the grumpy supervision of Susan Calvin.

Madarian's brilliance was quite obvious and Susan Calvin had quietly promoted him over the heads of older men. She wouldn't, in any case, have deigned to give her reasons for this to Research Director Peter Bogert, but as it happened, no reasons were needed. Or, rather, they were obvious.

Madarian was utterly the reverse of the renowned Dr. Calvin in several very noticeable ways. He was not quite as overweight as his distinct double chin made him appear to be, but even so he was overpowering in his presence, where Susan had gone nearly unnoticed. Madarian's massive face, his shock of glistening red-brown hair, his ruddy complexion and booming voice, his loud laugh, and most of all, his irrepressible self-confidence and his eager way of announcing his successes, made everyone else in the room feel there was a shortage of space.

When Susan Calvin finally retired (refusing, in advance, any cooperation with respect to any testimonial dinner that might be planned in her honor, with so firm a manner that no announcement of the retirement was even made to the news services) Madarian took her place.

He had been in his new post exactly one day when he initiated the JN project.

It had meant the largest commitment of funds to one project that United States Robots had ever had to weigh, but that was something which Madarian dismissed with a genial wave of the hand.

"Worth every penny of it, Peter," he said. "And I expect you to convince the Board of Directors of that."

"Give me reasons," said Bogert, wondering if Madarian would. Susan Calvin had never given reasons.

But Madarian said, "Sure," and settled himself easily into the large armchair in the Director's office.

Bogert watched the other with something that was almost awe. His own once-black hair was almost white now and within the decade he would follow Susan into retirement. That would mean the end of the original team that had built United States Robots into a globe-girdling firm that was a rival of the national governments in complexity and importance. Somehow neither he nor those who had gone before him ever quite grasped the enormous expansion of the firm.

But this was a new generation. The new men were at ease with the Colossus. They lacked the touch of wonder that would have them tiptoeing in disbelief. So they moved ahead, and that was good.

Madarian said, "I propose to begin the construction of robots without constraint."

"Without the Three Laws? Surely—"

"No, Peter. Are those the only constraints you can think

of. Hell, you contributed to the design of the early positronic brains. Do I have to tell you that, quite aside from the Three Laws, there isn't a pathway in those brains that isn't carefully designed and fixed? We have robots planned for specific tasks, implanted with specific abilities."

"And you propose—"

"That at every level below the Three Laws, the paths be made open-ended. It's not difficult."

Bogert said dryly, "It's not difficult, indeed. Useless things are never difficult. The difficult thing is fixing the paths and making the robot useful."

"But why is that difficult? Fixing the paths requires a great deal of effort because the Principle of Uncertainty is important in particles the mass of positrons and the uncertainty effect must be minimized. Yet why must it? If we arrange to have the Principle just sufficiently prominent to allow the crossing of paths unpredictably—"

"We have an unpredictable robot."

"We have a *creative* robot," said Madarian, with a trace of impatience. "Peter, if there's anything a human brain has that a robotic brain has never had, it's the trace of unpredictability that comes from the effects of uncertainty at the subatomic level. I admit that this effect has never been demonstrated experimentally within the nervous system, but without that the human brain is not superior to the robotic brain in principle."

"And you think that if you introduce the effect into the robotic brain, the human brain will become not superior to the robotic brain in principle."

"That," said Madarian, "is exactly what I believe."

They went on for a long time after that.

The Board of Directors clearly had no intention of being easily convinced.

Scott Robertson, the largest shareholder in the firm, said,

"It's hard enough to manage the robot industry as it is, with public hostility to robots forever on the verge of breaking out into the open. If the public gets the idea that robots will be uncontrolled . . . Oh, don't tell me about the Three Laws. The average man won't believe the Three Laws will protect him if he as much as hears the word 'uncontrolled.'"

"Then don't use it," said Madarian. "Call the robot—call it 'intuitive.'"

"An intuitive robot," someone muttered. "A girl robot?"

A smile made its way about the conference table.

Madarian seized on that. "All right. A girl robot. Our robots are sexless, of course, and so will this one be, but we always act as though they're males. We give them male pet names and call them he and him. Now this one, if we consider the nature of the mathematical structuring of the brain which I have proposed, would fall into the JN-coordinate system. The first robot would be JN-1, and I've assumed that it would be called John-1 . . . I'm afraid that is the level of originality of the average roboticist. But why not call it Jane-1, damn it? If the public has to be let in on what we're doing, we're constructing a feminine robot with intuition."

Robertson shook his head, "What difference would that make? What you're saying is that you plan to remove the last barrier which, in principle, keeps the robotic brain inferior to the human brain. What do you suppose the public reaction will be to that?"

"Do you plan to make that public?" said Madarian. He thought a bit and then said, "Look. One thing the general public believes is that women are not as intelligent as men."

There was an instant apprehensive look on the face of more than one man at the table and a quick look up and down as though Susan Calvin were still in her accustomed seat.

Madarian said, "If we announce a female robot, it doesn't matter what she is. The public will automatically assume she is mentally backward. We just publicize the robot as Jane-1 and we don't have to say another word. We're safe."

"Actually," said Peter Bogert quietly, "there's more to it than that. Madarian and I have gone over the mathematics carefully and the JN series, whether John or Jane, would be quite safe. They would be less complex and intellectually capable, in an orthodox sense, than many another series we have designed and constructed. There would only be the one added factor of, well, let's get into the habit of calling it 'intuition.'"

"Who knows what it would do?" muttered Robertson.

"Madarian has suggested one thing it can do. As you all know, the Space Jump has been developed in principle. It is possible for men to attain what is, in effect, hyper-speeds beyond that of light and to visit other stellar systems and return in negligible time—weeks at the most."

Robertson said, "That's not new to us. It couldn't have been done without robots."

"Exactly, and it's not doing us any good because we can't use the hyper-speed drive except perhaps once as a demonstration, so that U.S. Robots gets little credit. The Space Jump is risky, it's fearfully prodigal of energy and therefore it's enormously expensive. If we were going to use it anyway, it would be nice if we could report the existence of a habitable planet. Call it a psychological need. Spend about twenty billion dollars on a single Space Jump and report nothing but scientific data and the public wants to know why their money was wasted. Report the existence of a habitable planet, and you're an interstellar Columbus and no one will worry about the money."

"So?"

"So where are we going to find a habitable planet? Or put it this way—which star within reach of the Space Jump as presently developed, which of the three hundred thousand stars and star systems within three hundred light-years has the best chance of having a habitable planet? We've got an enormous quantity of details on every star in our three-hundred-light-year neighborhood and a notion that almost every one has a planetary system. But which has a *habitable* planet? Which do we visit? . . . We don't know."

One of the directors said, "How would this Jane robot help us?"

Madarian was about to answer that, but he gestured slightly to Bogert and Bogert understood. The Director would carry more weight. Bogert didn't particularly like the idea; if the JN series proved a fiasco, he was making himself prominent enough in connection with it to insure that the sticky fingers of blame would cling to him. On the other hand, retirement was not all that far off, and if it worked, he would go out in a blaze of glory. Maybe it was only Madarian's aura of confidence, but Bogert had honestly come to believe it would work.

He said, "It may well be that somewhere in the libraries of data we have on those stars, there are methods for estimating the probabilities of the presence of Earth-type habitable planets. All we need to do is understand the data properly, look at them in the appropriate creative manner, make the correct correlations. We haven't done it yet. Or if some astronomer has, he hasn't been smart enough to realize what he has.

"A JN-type robot could make correlations far more rapidly and far more precisely than a man could. In a day, it would make and discard as many correlations as a man could in ten years. Furthermore, it would work in truly random fashion, whereas a man would have a strong bias based on preconception and on what is already believed."

There was a considerable silence after that. Finally Robertson said, "But it's only a matter of probability, isn't it? Suppose this robot said, 'The highest-probability habitable-planet star within so-and-so light-years is Squidgee-17,' or whatever, and we go there and find that a probability is only a probability and that there are no habitable planets after all. Where does that leave us?"

Madarian struck in this time. "We still win. We know how the robot came to the conclusion because it—she—will tell us. It might well help us gain enormous insight into astronomical detail and make the whole thing worthwhile even if we don't make the Space Jump at all. Besides, we can then work out the five most probable sites of planets and the probability that one of the five has a habitable planet may then be better than 0.95. It would be almost sure—"

They went on for a long time after that.

The funds granted were quite insufficient, but Madarian counted on the habit of throwing good money after bad. With two hundred million about to be lost irrevocably when another hundred million could save everything, the other hundred million would surely be voted.

Jane-1 was finally built and put on display. Peter Bogert studied it—her—gravely. He said, "Why the narrow waist? Surely that introduces a mechanical weakness?"

Madarian chuckled. "Listen, if we're going to call her Jane, there's no point in making her look like Tarzan."

Bogert shook his head. "Don't like it. You'll be bulging her higher up to give the appearance of breasts next, and that's a rotten idea. If women start getting the notion that robots may look like women, I can tell you exactly the kind of perverse notions they'll get, and you'll *really* have hostility on their part."

Madarian said, "Maybe you're right at that. No woman wants to feel replaceable by something with none of her faults. Okay."

• • •

Jane-2 did not have the pinched waist. She was a somber robot which rarely moved and even more rarely spoke.

Madarian had only occasionally come rushing to Bogert with items of news during her construction and that had been a sure sign that things were going poorly. Madarian's ebullience under success was overpowering. He would not hesitate to invade Bogert's bedroom at 3 A.M. with a hot-flash item rather than wait for the morning. Bogert was sure of that.

Now Madarian seemed subdued, his usually florid expression nearly pale, his round cheeks somehow pinched. Bogert said, with a feeling of certainty, "She won't talk."

"Oh, she talks." Madarian sat down heavily and chewed at his lower lip. "Sometimes, anyway," he said.

Bogert rose and circled the robot. "And when she talks, she makes no sense, I suppose. Well, if she doesn't talk, she's no female, is she?"

Madarian tried a weak smile for size and abandoned it. He said, "The brain, in isolation, checked out."

"I know," said Bogert.

"But once that brain was put in charge of the physical apparatus of the robot, it was necessarily modified, of course."

"Of course," agreed Bogert unhelpfully.

"But unpredictably and frustratingly. The trouble is that when you're dealing with n-dimensional calculus of uncertainty, things are—"

"Uncertain?" said Bogert. His own reaction was surprising him. The company investment was already most sizable and almost two years had elapsed, yet the results were, to put it politely, disappointing. Still, he found himself jabbing at Madarian and finding himself amused in the process.

Almost furtively, Bogert wondered if it weren't the absent Susan Calvin he was jabbing at. Madarian was so much more ebullient and effusive than Susan could ever possibly be—when things were going well. He was also far more vulnerably in the dumps when things weren't going well, and it was precisely under pressure that Susan never cracked. The target that Madarian made could be a neatly punctured bull's-eye as recompense for the target Susan had never allowed herself to be.

Madarian did not react to Bogert's last remark any more than Susan Calvin would have done; not out of contempt, which would have been Susan's reaction, but because he did not hear it.

He said argumentatively, "The trouble is the matter of recognition. We have Jane-2 correlating magnificently. She can correlate on any subject, but once she's done so, she can't recognize a valuable result from a valueless one. It's not an easy problem, judging how to program a robot to tell a significant correlation when you don't know what correlations she will be making."

"I presume you've thought of lowering the potential at the W-21 diode junction and sparking across the—"

"No, no, no, no—" Madarian faded off into a whispering diminuendo. "You can't just have it spew out everything. We can do that ourselves. The point is to have it recognize the crucial correlation and draw the conclusion. Once that is done, you see, a Jane robot would snap out an answer by intuition. It would be something we couldn't get ourselves except by the oddest kind of luck."

"It seems to me," said Bogert dryly, "that if you had a robot like that, you would have her do routinely what, among human beings, only the occasional genius is capable of doing."

Madarian nodded vigorously. "Exactly, Peter. I'd have said so myself if I weren't afraid of frightening off the execs. Please don't repeat that in their hearing."

"Do you really want a robot genius?"

"What are words? I'm trying to get a robot with the capacity to make random correlations at enormous speeds, together with a key-significance high-recognition quotient. And I'm trying to put *those* words into positronic field equations. I thought I had it, too, but I don't. Not yet."

He looked at Jane-2 discontentedly and said, "What's the best significance you have, Jane?"

Jane-2's head turned to look at Madarian but she made no sound, and Madarian whispered with resignation, "She's running that into the correlation banks."

Jane-2 spoke tonelessly at last. "I'm not sure." It was the first sound she had made.

Madarian's eyes rolled upward. "She's doing the equivalent of setting up equations with indeterminate solutions."

"I gathered that," said Bogert. "Listen, Madarian, can you go anywhere at this point, or do we pull out now and cut our losses at half a billion?"

"Oh, I'll get it," muttered Madarian.

Jane-3 wasn't it. She was never as much as activated and Madarian was in a rage.

It was human error. His own fault, if one wanted to be entirely accurate. Yet though Madarian was utterly humiliated, others remained quiet. Let he who has never made an error in the fearsomely intricate mathematics of the positronic brain fill out the first memo of correction.

Nearly a year passed before Jane-4 was ready. Madarian was ebullient again. "She does it," he said. "She's got a good high-recognition quotient."

He was confident enough to place her on display before the Board and have her solve problems. Not mathematical problems; any robot could do that; but problems where the terms were deliberately misleading without being actually inaccurate.

Bogert said afterward, "That doesn't take much, really."

"Of course not. It's elementary for Jane-4, but I had to show them something, didn't I?"

"Do you know how much we've spent so far?"

"Come on, Peter, don't give me that. Do you know how much we've got back? These things don't go on in a vacuum, you know. I've had over three years of hell over this, if you want to know, but I've worked out new techniques of calculation that will save us a minimum of fifty thousand dollars on every new type of positronic brain we design, from now on in forever. Right?"

"Well—"

"Well me no wells. It's so. And it's my personal feeling that n-dimensional calculus of uncertainty can have any number of other applications if we have the ingenuity to find them, and my Jane robots *will* find them. Once I've got exactly what I want, the new JN series will pay for itself inside of five years, even if we triple what we've invested so far."

"What do you mean by 'exactly what you want'? What's wrong with Jane-4?"

"Nothing. Or nothing much. She's on the track, but she can be improved and I intend to do so. I thought I knew where I was going when I designed her. Now I've tested her and I *know* where I'm going. I intend to get there."

Jane-5 was it. It took Madarian well over a year to produce her and there he had no reservations; he was utterly confident.

Jane-5 was shorter than the average robot, slimmer. Without being a female caricature as Jane-1 had been, she managed to possess an air of femininity about herself despite the absence of a single clearly feminine feature.

"It's the way she's standing," said Bogert. Her arms were held gracefully and somehow the torso managed to give the impression of curving slightly when she turned.

Madarian said, "Listen to her . . . How do you feel, Jane?"

"In excellent health, thank you," said Jane-5, and the voice was precisely that of a woman; it was a sweet and almost disturbing contralto.

"Why did you do that, Clinton?" said Peter, startled and beginning to frown.

"Psychologically important," said Madarian. "I want people to think of her as a woman; to treat her as a woman; to *explain*."

"What people?"

Madarian put his hands in his pockets and stared thoughtfully at Bogert. "I would like to have arrangements made for Jane and myself to go to Flagstaff."

Bogert couldn't help but note that Madarian didn't say Jane-5. He made use of no number this time. She was *the* Jane. He said doubtfully, "To Flagstaff? Why?"

"Because that's the world center for general planetology, isn't it? It's where they're studying the stars and trying to calculate the probability of habitable planets, isn't it?"

"I know that, but it's on Earth."

"Well, and I surely know that."

"Robotic movements on Earth are strictly controlled. And there's no need for it. Bring a library of books on general planetology here and let Jane absorb them."

"*No!* Peter, will you get it through your head that Jane isn't the ordinary logical robot; she's intuitive."

"So?"

"So how can we tell what she needs, what she can use, what will set her off? We can use any metal model in the factory to read books; that's frozen data and out of date besides. Jane must have living information; she must have tones of voice, she must have side issues; she must have total irrelevancies even. How the devil do we know what or when something will go click-click inside her and fall into a pattern? If we knew, we wouldn't need her at all, would we?"

Bogert began to feel harassed. He said, "Then bring the men here, the general planetologists."

"Here won't be any good. They'll be out of their element. They won't react naturally. I want Jane to watch them at work; I want her to see their instruments, their offices, their desks, everything about them that she can. I want you to arrange to have her transported to Flagstaff. And I'd really like not to discuss it any further."

For a moment he almost sounded like Susan. Bogert winced, and said, "It's complicated making such an arrangement. Transporting an experimental robot—"

"Jane isn't experimental. She's the fifth of the series."

"The other four weren't really working models."

Madarian lifted his hands in helpless frustration. "Who's forcing you to tell the government that?"

"I'm not worried about the government. It can be made to understand special cases. It's public opinion. We've come a long way in fifty years and I don't propose to be set back twenty-five of them by having you lose control of a—"

"I won't lose control. You're making foolish remarks. Look! U.S. Robots can afford a private plane. We can land quietly at the nearest commercial airport and be lost in hundreds of similar landings. We can arrange to have a large ground car with an enclosed body meet us and take us to Flagstaff. Jane will be crated and it will be obvious that some piece of thoroughly non-robotic equipment is being transported to the labs. We won't get a second look from anyone. The men at Flagstaff will be alerted and will be told the exact purpose of the visit. They will have every motive to cooperate and to prevent a leak."

Bogert pondered. "The risky part will be the plane and the ground car. If anything happens to the crate—"

"Nothing will."

"We might get away with it if Jane is deactivated during transport. Then even if someone finds out she's inside—"

"No, Peter. That can't be done. Uh-uh. Not Jane-5. Look, she's been free-associating since she was activated. The information she possesses can be put into freeze during deactivation but the free associations never. No, sir, she can't ever be deactivated."

"But, then, if somehow it is discovered that we are transporting an activated robot—"

"It won't be found out."

Madarian remained firm and the plane eventually took off. It was a late-model automatic Computo-jet, but it carried a human pilot—one of U. S. Robots' own employees—as backup. The crate containing Jane arrived at the airport safely, was transferred to the ground car, and reached the Research Laboratories at Flagstaff without incident.

Peter Bogert received his first call from Madarian not more than an hour after the latter's arrival at Flagstaff. Madarian was ecstatic and, characteristically, could not wait to report.

The message arrived by tubed laser beam, shielded, scrambled, and ordinarily impenetrable, but Bogert felt exasperated. He knew it could be penetrated if someone with enough technological ability—the government, for example—was determined to do so. The only real safety lay in the fact that the government had no reason to try. At least Bogert hoped so.

He said, "For God's sake, do you have to call?"

Madarian ignored him entirely. He burbled, "It was an inspiration. Sheer genius, I tell you."

For a while, Bogert stared at the receiver. Then he shouted incredulously, "You mean you've got the answer? Already?"

"No, no! Give us time, damn it. I mean the matter of her

voice was an inspiration. Listen, after we were chauffeured from the airport to the main administration building at Flagstaff, we uncrated Jane and she stepped out of the box. When that happened, every man in the place stepped back. Scared! Nitwits! If even scientists can't understand the significance of the Laws of Robotics, what can we expect of the average untrained individual? For a minute there I thought: This will all be useless. They won't talk. They'll be keying themselves for a quick break in case she goes berserk and they'll be able to think of nothing else."

"Well, then, what are you getting at?"

"So then she greeted them routinely. She said, 'Good afternoon, gentlemen. I am so glad to meet you.' And it came out in this beautiful contralto . . . That was it. One man straightened his tie, and another ran his fingers through his hair. What really got me was that the oldest guy in the place actually checked his fly to make sure it was zipped. They're all crazy about her now. All they needed was the voice. She isn't a robot any more; she's a girl."

"You mean they're talking to her?"

"*Are* they talking to her! I should say so. I should have programmed her for sexy intonations. They'd be asking her for dates right now if I had. Talk about conditioned reflex. Listen, men respond to voices. At the most intimate moments, are they looking? It's the voice in your ear—"

"Yes, Clinton, I seem to remember. Where's Jane now?"

"With them. They won't let go of her."

"Damn! Get in there with her. Don't let her out of your sight, man."

Madarian's calls thereafter, during his ten-day stay at Flagstaff, were not very frequent and became progressively less exalted.

Jane was listening carefully, he reported, and occasionally she responded. She remained popular. She was given entry everywhere. But there were no results.

Bogert said, "Nothing at all?"

Madarian was at once defensive. "You can't say nothing at all. It's impossible to say nothing at all with an intuitive robot. You don't know what might not be going on inside her. This morning she asked Jensen what he had for breakfast."

"Rossiter Jensen the astrophysicist?"

"Yes, of course. As it turned out, he didn't have breakfast that morning. Well, a cup of coffee."

"So Jane's learning to make small talk. That scarcely makes up for the expense—"

"Oh, don't be a jackass. It wasn't small talk. Nothing is small talk for Jane. She asked because it had something to do with some sort of cross-correlation she was building in her mind."

"What can it possibly—"

"How do I know? If I knew, I'd be a Jane myself and you wouldn't need her. But it has to mean something. She's programmed for high motivation to obtain an answer to the question of a planet with optimum habitability/distance and—"

"Then let me know when she's done that and not before. It's not really necessary for me to get a blow-by-blow description of possible correlations."

He didn't really expect to get notification of success. With each day, Bogert grew less sanguine, so that when the notification finally came, he wasn't ready. And it came at the very end.

That last time, when Madarian's climactic message came, it came in what was almost a whisper. Exaltation had come complete circle and Madarian was awed into quiet.

"She did it," he said. "She did it. After I all but gave up, too. After she had received everything in the place and most of it twice and three times over and never said a word that sounded like anything . . . I'm on the plane now, returning. We've just taken off."

Bogert managed to get his breath. "Don't play games, man. You have the *answer?* Say so, if you have. Say it plainly."

"She has the answer. She's given me the answer. She's given me the names of three stars within eighty light-years which, she says, have a sixty to ninety per cent chance of possessing one habitable planet each. The probability that at least one has is 0.972. It's almost certain. And that's just the least of it. Once we get back, she can give us the exact line of reasoning that led her to the conclusion and I predict that the whole science of astrophysics and cosmology will—"

"Are you sure—"

"You think I'm having hallucinations? I even have a witness. Poor guy jumped two feet when Jane suddenly began to reel out the answer in her gorgeous voice—"

And that was when the meteorite struck and in the thorough destruction of the plane that followed, Madarian and the pilot were reduced to gobbets of bloody flesh and no usable remnant of Jane was recovered.

The gloom at U. S. Robots had never been deeper. Robertson attempted to find consolation in the fact that the very completeness of the destruction had utterly hidden the illegalities of which the firm had been guilty.

Peter shook his head and mourned. "We've lost the best chance U.S. Robots ever had of gaining an unbeatable public image; of overcoming the damned Frankenstein complex. What it would have meant for robots to have one of them work out the solution to the habitable-planet problem, after other robots had helped work out the Space Jump. Robots would have opened the galaxy to us. And if at the same time we could have driven scientific knowledge forward in a dozen different directions as we surely would have . . . Oh, God, there's no way of calculating the benefits to the human race, and to us of course."

Robertson said, "We could build other Janes, couldn't we? Even without Madarian?"

"Sure we could. But can we depend on the proper correlation again? Who knows how low-probability that final result was? What if Madarian had had a fantastic piece of beginner's luck? And then to have an even more fantastic piece of bad luck? A meteorite zeroing in . . . It's simply unbelievable—"

Robertson said in a hesitating whisper, "It couldn't have been—meant. I mean, if we weren't meant to know and if the meteorite was a judgment—from—"

He faded off under Bogert's withering glare.

Bogert said, "It's not a dead loss, I suppose. Other Janes are bound to help us in some ways. And we can give other robots feminine voices, if that will help encourage public acceptance—though I wonder what the women would say. If we only knew what Jane-5 had said!"

"In that last call, Madarian said there was a witness."

Bogert said, "I know; I've been thinking about that. Don't you suppose I've been in touch with Flagstaff? Nobody in the entire place heard Jane say anything that was out of the ordinary, anything that sounded like an answer to the habitable-planet problem, and certainly anyone there should have recognized the answer if it came—or at least recognized it as a possible answer."

"Could Madarian have been lying? Or crazy? Could he have been trying to protect himself—"

"You mean he may have been trying to save his reputation by pretending he had the answer and then gimmick Jane so she couldn't talk and say, 'Oh, sorry, something happened accidentally. Oh, darn!' I won't accept that for a minute. You might as well suppose he had arranged the meteorite."

"Then what do we do?"

Bogert said heavily, "Turn back to Flagstaff. The answer *must* be there. I've got to dig deeper, that's all. I'm going there and I'm taking a couple of the men in Madarian's department. We've got to go through that place top to bottom and end to end."

"But, you know, even if there were a witness and he had heard, what good would it do, now that we don't have Jane to explain the process?"

"Every little something is useful. Jane gave the names of the stars; the catalogue numbers probably—none of the named stars has a chance. If someone can remember her saying that and actually remember the catalogue number, or have heard it clearly enough to allow it to be recovered by Psycho-probe if he lacked the conscious memory—then we'll have something. Given the results at the end, and the data fed Jane at the beginning, we might be able to reconstruct the line of reasoning; we might recover the intuition. If that is done, we've saved the game—"

Bogert was back after three days, silent and thoroughly depressed. When Robertson inquired anxiously as to results, he shook his head. "Nothing!"

"Nothing?"

"Absolutely nothing. I spoke with every man in Flagstaff—every scientist, every technician, every student—that had had anything to do with Jane; everyone that had as much as seen her. The number wasn't great; I'll give Madarian credit for that much discretion. He only allowed those to see her who might conceivably have had planetological knowledge to feed her. There were twenty-three men altogether who had seen Jane and of those only twelve had spoken to her more than casually.

"I went over and over all that Jane had said. They remembered everything quite well. They're keen men engaged in a crucial experiment involving their specialty, so they had every motivation to remember. And they were dealing with a talking robot, something that was startling enough, and one that talked like a TV actress. They couldn't forget."

Robertson said, "Maybe a Psycho-probe—"

"If one of them had the vaguest thought that something had happened, I would screw out his consent to Probing. But there's nothing to leave room for an excuse, and to Probe two dozen men who make their living from their brains can't be done. Honestly, it wouldn't help. If Jane had mentioned three stars and said they had habitable planets, it would have been like setting up sky rockets in their brains. How could any one of them forget?"

"Then maybe one of them is lying," said Robertson grimly. "He wants the information for his own use; to get the credit himself later."

"What good would that do him?" said Bogert. "The whole establishment knows exactly why Madarian and Jane were there in the first place. They know why I came there in the second. If at any time in the future any man now at Flagstaff suddenly comes up with a habitable-planet theory that is startlingly new and different, yet valid, every other man at Flagstaff and every man at U. S. Robots will know at once that he had stolen it. He'd never get away with it."

"Then Madarian himself was somehow mistaken."

"I don't see how I can believe that either. Madarian had an irritating personality—all robopsychologists have irritating personalities, I think, which must be why they work with robots rather than with men—but he was no dummy. He *couldn't* be wrong in something like this."

"Then—" But Robertson had run out of possibilities.

They had reached a blank wall and for some minutes each stared at it disconsolately.

Finally Robertson stirred. "Peter—"

"Well?"

"Let's ask Susan."

Bogert stiffened. "What!"

"Let's ask Susan. Let's call her and ask her to come in."

"Why? What can she possibly do?"

"I don't know. But she's a robopsychologist, too, and she might understand Madarian better than we do. Besides, she— Oh, hell, she always had more brains than any of us."

"She's nearly eighty."

"And you're seventy. What about it?"

Bogert sighed. Had her abrasive tongue lost any of its rasp in the years of her retirement? He said, "Well, I'll ask her."

Susan Calvin entered Bogert's office with a slow look around before her eyes fixed themselves on the Research Director. She had aged a great deal since her retirement. Her hair was a fine white and her face seemed to have crumpled. She had grown so frail as to be almost transparent and only her eyes, piercing and uncompromising, seemed to remain of all that had been.

Bogert strode forward heartily, holding out his hand. "Susan!"

Susan Calvin took it, and said, "You're looking reasonably well, Peter, for an old man. If I were you, I wouldn't wait till next year. Retire now and let the young men get to it . . . And Madarian is dead. Are you calling me in to take over my old job? Are you determined to keep the ancients till a year past actual physical death?"

"No, no, Susan. I've called you in—" He stopped. He did not, after all, have the faintest idea of how to start.

But Susan read his mind now as easily as she always had.

She seated herself with the caution born of stiffened joints and said, "Peter, you've called me in because you're in bad trouble. Otherwise you'd sooner see me dead than within a mile of you."

"Come, Susan—"

"Don't waste time on pretty talk. I never had time to waste when I was forty and certainly not now. Madarian's death and your call to me are both unusual, so there must be a connection. Two unusual events without a connection is too low-probability to worry about. Begin at the beginning and don't worry about revealing yourself to be a fool. That was revealed to me long ago."

Bogert cleared his throat miserably and began. She listened carefully, her withered hand lifting once in a while to stop him so that she might ask a question.

She snorted at one point. "Feminine intuition? Is that what you wanted the robot for? You men. Faced with a woman reaching a correct conclusion and unable to accept the fact that she is your equal or superior in intelligence, you invent something called feminine intuition."

"Uh, yes, Susan, but let me continue—"

He did. When she was told of Jane's contralto voice, she said, "It is a difficult choice sometimes whether to feel revolted at the male sex or merely to dismiss them as contemptible."

Bogert said, "Well, let me go on—"

When he was quite done, Susan said, "May I have the private use of this office for an hour or two?"

"Yes, but—"

She said, "I want to go over the various records—Jane's programming, Madarian's calls, your interviews at Flagstaff. I presume I can use that beautiful new shielded laserphone and your computer outlet if I wish."

"Yes, of course."

"Well, then, get out of here, Peter."

• • •

It was not quite forty-five minutes when she hobbled to the door, opened it, and called for Bogert.

When Bogert came, Robertson was with him. Both entered and Susan greeted the latter with an unenthusiastic "Hello, Scott."

Bogert tried desperately to gauge the results from Susan's face, but it was only the face of a grim old lady who had no intention of making anything easy for him.

He said cautiously, "Do you think there's anything you can do, Susan?"

"Beyond what I have already done? No! There's nothing more."

Bogert's lips set in chagrin, but Robertson said, "What have you already done, Susan?"

Susan said, "I've thought a little; something I can't seem to persuade anyone else to do. For one thing, I've thought about Madarian. I knew him, you know. He had brains but he was a very irritating extrovert. I thought you would like him after me, Peter."

"It was a change," Bogert couldn't resist saying.

"And he was always running to you with results the very minute he had them, wasn't he?"

"Yes, he was."

"And yet," said Susan, "his last message, the one in which he said Jane had given him the answer, was sent from the plane. Why did he wait so long? Why didn't he call you while he was still at Flagstaff, immediately after Jane had said whatever it was she said?"

"I suppose," said Peter, "that for once he wanted to check it thoroughly and—well, I don't know. It was the most important thing that had ever happened to him; he might for once have wanted to wait and be sure of himself."

"On the contrary; the more important it was, the less he would wait, surely. And if he could manage to wait, why not do it properly and wait till he was back at U. S. Robots so that he could check the results with all the computing equipment this firm could make available to him? In short, he waited too long from one point of view and not long enough from another."

Robertson interrupted. "Then you think he was up to some trickery—"

Susan looked revolted. "Scott, don't try to compete with Peter in making inane remarks. Let me continue . . . A second point concerns the witness. According to the records of that last call, Madarian said, 'Poor guy jumped two feet when Jane suddenly began to reel out the answer in her gorgeous voice.' In fact, it was the last thing he said. And the question is, then, why should the witness have jumped? Madarian had explained that all the men were crazy about that voice, and they had had ten days with the robot—with Jane. Why should the mere act of her speaking have startled them?"

Bogert said, "I assumed it was astonishment at hearing Jane give an answer to a problem that has occupied the minds of planetologists for nearly a century."

"But they were *waiting* for her to give that answer. That was why she was there. Besides, consider the way the sentence is worded. Madarian's statement makes it seem the witness was startled, not astonished, if you see the difference. What's more, that reaction came 'when Jane suddenly began'—in other words, at the very start of the statement. To be astonished at the content of what Jane said would have required the witness to have listened awhile so that he might absorb it. Madarian would have said he had jumped two feet *after* he had heard Jane say thus-and-so. It would be 'after' not 'when' and the word 'suddenly' would not be included."

Bogert said uneasily, "I don't think you can refine matters down to the use or non-use of a word."

"I can," said Susan frostily, "because I am a robopsychologist. And I can expect Madarian to do so, too, because *he* was a robopsychologist. We have to explain those two anomalies, then. The queer delay before Madarian's call and the queer reaction of the witness."

"Can *you* explain them?" asked Robertson.

"Of course," said Susan, "since I use a little simple logic. Madarian called with the news without delay, as he always did, or with as little delay as he could manage. If Jane had solved the problem at Flagstaff, he would certainly have called from Flagstaff. Since he called from the plane, she must clearly have solved the problem after he had left Flagstaff."

"But then—"

"Let me finish. Let me finish. Was Madarian not taken from the airport to Flagstaff in a heavy, enclosed ground car? And Jane, in her crate, with him?"

"Yes."

"And presumably, Madarian and the crated Jane returned from Flagstaff to the airport in the same heavy, enclosed ground car. Am I right?"

"Yes, of course!"

"And they were not alone in the ground car, either. In one of his calls, Madarian said, 'We were chauffeured from the airport to the main administration building,' and I suppose I am right in concluding that if he was chauffeured, then that was because there was a chauffeur, a human driver, in the car."

"Good God!"

"The trouble with you, Peter, is that when you think of a witness to a planetological statement, you think of planetologists. You divide up human beings into categories, and despise and dismiss most. A robot cannot do that. The First Law says, 'A robot may not injure a *human being* or, through inaction, allow a *human being* to come to harm.'

Any human being. That is the essence of the robotic view of life. A robot makes no distinction. To a robot, all men are truly equal, and to a robopsychologist who must perforce deal with men at the robotic level, all men are truly equal, too.

"It would not occur to Madarian to say a truck driver had heard the statement. To you a truck driver is not a scientist but is a mere animate adjunct of a truck, but to Madarian he was a man and a witness. Nothing more. Nothing less."

Bogert shook his head in disbelief, "But you are *sure?*"

"Of course I'm sure. How else can you explain the other point; Madarian's remark about the startling of the witness? Jane was crated, wasn't she? But she was *not* deactivated. According to the records, Madarian was always adamant against ever deactivating an intuitive robot. Moreover, Jane-5, like any of the Janes, was extremely non-talkative. Probably it never occurred to Madarian to order her to remain quiet within the crate; and it was within the crate that the pattern finally fell into place. Naturally she began to talk. A beautiful contralto voice suddenly sounded from inside the crate. If you were the truck driver, what would you do at that point? Surely you'd be startled. It's a wonder he didn't crash."

"But if the truck driver was the witness, why didn't he come forward—"

"Why? Can he possibly know that anything crucial had happened, that what he heard was important? Besides, don't you suppose Madarian tipped him well and asked him not to say anything? Would you *want* the news to spread that an activated robot was being transported illegally over the Earth's surface."

"Well, will he remember what was said?"

"Why not? It might seem to you, Peter, that a truck driver, one step above an ape in your view, can't remember. But truck drivers can have brains, too. The statements were most remarkable and the driver may well have remembered some. Even if he gets some of the letters and numbers wrong, we're dealing with a finite set, you know, the fifty-five hundred stars or star systems within eighty light-years or so—I haven't looked up the exact number. You can make the correct choices. And if needed, you will have every excuse to use the Psycho-probe—"

The two men stared at her. Finally Bogert, afraid to believe, whispered, "But how can you be *sure*?"

For a moment, Susan was on the point of saying: Because I've called Flagstaff, you fool, and because I spoke to the truck driver, and because he told me what he had heard, and because I've checked with the computer at Flagstaff and got the only three stars that fit the information, and because I have those names in my pocket.

But she didn't. Let him go through it all himself. Carefully, she rose to her feet, and said sardonically, "How can I be sure? . . . Call it feminine intuition."

A PROBLEM OF NUMBERS

Professor Neddring looked mildly at his graduate student. The young man sat there at ease; his hair was a little on the reddish side, his eyes were keen but calm, and his hands rested in the pockets of his lab coat. Altogether a promising specimen, the professor thought.

He had known for some time that the boy was interested in his daughter. What was more to the point, he had known for some time his daughter was interested in the boy.

The professor said, "Let's get this straight, Hal. You've come to me for my approval before you propose to my daughter?"

Hal Kemp said, "That's right, sir."

"Granted that I'm not up on the latest fads of youth—but surely this can't be the new 'in' thing." The professor thrust his hands into his lab coat pockets and leaned back in his chair. "Surely, young people aren't taking to asking permission these days? Don't tell me you'll give up my daughter if I turn you down?"

"No, not if she'll still have me, and I think she will. But it would be pleasant—"

"—if you had my approval. Why?"

Hal said, "For very practical reasons. I don't have my doctor's degree yet and I don't want it said that I'm dating your daughter to help me get it. If you think I am, say so, and maybe I'll wait till after I get my degree. Or maybe I won't and take my chances that your disapproval will make it that much harder for me to get my degree."

"So, for the sake of your doctorate, you think it would be nice if we were friends about your marriage to Janice."

"To be honest, yes, Professor."

There was silence between them. Professor Neddring thought about the matter with a certain creakiness. His research work for some years now had dealt with the coordination complexes of chromium and there was a definite difficulty in thinking with some precision about anything as imprecise as affection and marriage.

He rubbed his smooth cheek—at the age of fifty he was too old for the various beard styles affected by the younger members of the department—and said, "Well, Hal, if you want a decision from me I'll have to base it on something, and the only way I know how to judge people is by their reasoning powers. My daughter judges you in *her* way, but I'll have to judge you in *mine*."

"Certainly," said Hal.

"Then let me put it this way." The professor leaned forward, scribbled something on a piece of paper, and said, "Tell me what this says, and you will have my blessing."

Hall picked up the paper. What was written on it was a series of numbers:

69663717263376833047

He said, "A cryptogram?"

"You can call it that."

Hal frowned slightly. "You mean you want me to solve a cryptogram and if I do, then you'll approve the marriage?"

"Yes."

"And if I don't, then you *won't* approve the marriage?"

"It may sound trivial, I admit, but this is my criterion. You can always marry without my approval. Janice is of age."

Hal shook his head. "I'd still rather have your approval. How much time do I have?"

"None. Tell me what it says *now*. Reason it out."

"*Now*?"

The professor nodded.

Hal Kemp shifted in his chair and stared at the row of numbers in his hand. "Do I figure it out in my head? Or can I use pencil and paper?"

"Just do it. Talk. Let me hear how you think. Who knows? If I like the way you think, I may give my approval even if you don't solve it."

Hal said, "Well, all right. It's a challenge. In the first place, I'll make an assumption. I'll assume you're an honorable man and would not set me a problem that you knew in advance I couldn't solve. Therefore this is a cryptogram which, to the best of your judgment, is one I can solve sitting in this chair and almost on the spur of the moment. Which in turn means that it involves something I know well."

"That sounds reasonable," agreed the professor.

But Hal wasn't listening. He continued, deliberately, "I know the alphabet well, of course, so this could be an ordinary substitution cipher—numbers for letters. Presumably, it would have to have some subtlety if it were, or it would be too easy. But I'm an amateur at that sort of thing and unless I can see at once some peculiar pattern in the numbers that gives the whole thing meaning, I'd be lost. I notice there are five 6's and five 3's and not a single 5—but that means nothing to me. So I'll abandon the possibility of a generalized cipher and move on to our own specialized field."

He thought again and went on, "Your specialized field, Professor, is inorganic chemistry and that, certainly, is what mine is going to be. And to any chemist, numbers immediately suggest atomic numbers. Every chemical element has its own number and there are one hundred and four elements known today; so the numbers involved would be 1 to 104.

"You haven't indicated how the numbers are divided up. There are the one-digit atomic numbers from 1 to 9; the two-digit ones from 10 to 99; and the three-digit ones from 100 to 104. This is all obvious, Professor, but you wanted to hear my reasoning, so I'm giving it to you in full.

"We can forget the three-digit atomic numbers, since in them a 1 is always followed by a 0 and the single 1 in your cryptogram is followed by a 7. Since you've given me twenty digits altogether, it is at least possible that only two-digit atomic numbers are involved—ten of them. There might be nine two-digit ones and two one-digit ones, but I doubt it. Even the presence of two one-digit atomic numbers could result in hundreds of different combinations of places in this list and that would surely make things too difficult for an instant or even a quick solution. It seems certain to me, then, that I am dealing with ten two-digit numbers, and we can therefore turn the message into: 69, 66, 37, 17, 26, 33, 76, 83, 30, 47.

"These numbers seem to mean nothing in themselves, but if they are atomic numbers then why not convert all of them into the names of the elements they represent? The names *might* be meaningful. That's not so easy offhand because I haven't memorized the list of elements in order of their atomic numbers. May I look them up in a table?"

The professor was listening with interest. "I didn't look up anything when I prepared the cryptogram."

"All right, then. Let's see," said Hal slowly. "Some are obvious. I know that 17 is chlorine, 26 is iron, 83 is bismuth, 30 is zinc. As for 76, that's somewhere near gold, which is 79; that would mean platinum, osimum, iridium. I'd say it means osmium. The other two are rare earth elements and I can never get those straight. Let's see—let's see—All right. I *think* I have them."

He wrote rapidly and said, "The list of the ten elements in your list is thulium, dysprosium, rubidium, chlorine, iron, arsenic, osmium, bismuth, zinc, and silver. Is that right?—No, don't answer."

He studied the list intently. "I see no connections among those elements, nothing that seems to give me any hint. Let's pass on then and ask if there is anything besides the atomic *number* that is so characteristic of elements that it would spring to any chemist's mind at once. Obviously, it would be the chemical *symbol*—the one-letter or two-letter abbreviation for each element that becomes second nature to any chemist. In this case the list of chemical symbols is"—he wrote again—"Tm, Dy, Rb, Cl, Fe, As, Os, Bi, Zn, Ag.

"These might form a word or sentence, but they don't, do they? So it would have to be a little more subtle than that. If you make an acrostic out of it and read just the first letters, that doesn't help, either. So if we try the next most obvious step and read the second letters of each symbol in order, we come out with 'my blessing.' I presume that's the solution, Professor."

"It is," said Professor Neddring gravely. "You reasoned it out with precision and you have my permission, for what that's worth, to propose to my daughter."

Hal rose, turned to leave, hesitated, then turned back. He said, "On the other hand, I don't like to take credit that's not mine. The reasoning I used may have been precise, but I offered it to you only because I wanted you to hear me reason logically. Actually, I knew the answer before I began, so in a way I cheated and I've got to admit that."

"Oh? How so?"

"Well, I know you think well of me and I guessed you would want me to come up with a solution and that you wouldn't be above giving me a hint. When you handed the cryptogram to me, you said, 'Tell me what this says, and you will have my blessing.' I guessed that you might mean that literally. 'My blessing' has ten letters and you handed me twenty digits. So I broke it down into ten pairs at once.

"Then, too, I told you I hadn't memorized the list of elements. The few elements I did remember were enough to show me that the second letters of the symbols were spelling out 'my blessing,' so I worked out the others from among those few that had the proper second letters in *their* symbols. Do I still make it?"

Professor Neddring finally smiled. He said, "Now, my boy, you *really* make it. Any competent scientist can think logically. The great ones use intuition."

BILL AND I

I am, as it happens, doing a book on Lord Byron's narrative poem *Don Juan*.* The poem is an uninhibited satire in which Byron takes the opportunity to lash out at everything and everyone that displeased him. He is cruel to the point of sadism toward Britain's monarchs, toward its poet laureate, toward its greatest general, and so on.

But those for whom he reserves his most savage sallies are his critics. Byron did not take to criticism kindly and he invariably struck back.

Now, as far as I know, there is no such thing as a writer who takes to criticism kindly. Most of us, however, affect stoic unconcern and bleed in private.

For myself, alas, stoic unconcern is impossible. My frank and ingenuous countenance is a blank page on which my every emotion is clearly written (I am told) and I don't think I have ever succeeded in playing the stoic for even half a second. Indeed, when I am criticized unfairly, everyone within earshot knows that I have been—and for as much as hours at a time.

*Because I want to, and because my publishers humor me.

Naturally, when I recently published a two-volume book entitled *Asimov's Guide to Shakespeare*, I tried to steel myself for inevitable events. It was bound to get into the hand of an occasional Shakespearian scholar who would come all over faint at the thought of someone outside their field daring to invade the sacred precincts.

In fact, the very first review I received began: "What is Isaac Asimov, spinner of outer-space tales, doing—"

Naturally, I read no further. The fact that I am a spinner of outer-space tales is utterly irrelevant to this particular book and can only be mentioned because the reviewer thinks there is something vaguely (or not so vaguely) beneath literary dignity in being a science fiction writer.

I have sought a printable response for that and failed, so I'll pass on.

A second review was much more interesting. It appeared in a Kentucky paper and was written by someone I will call Mr. X. It begins this way: "Isaac Asimov is associate professor of biochemistry at Boston University, and a prolific writer in many fields. I have read several of his books on science with the greatest attention and respect."

So far, so good. I am delighted.

But then, a very little while later, he says: "In this book, however, he has left the sunlit paths of natural science for the treacherous bogs of literature—"

What he objects to, it seems, is that I have annotated the plays, explained all the historical, legendary, and mythological references. It is a book of footnotes, so to speak, and he resents it. He points out that he thinks of "the language, the poetry, as the chief glory of Shakespeare's works."

Well, who doesn't? I'm delighted that Mr. X is clever enough to understand the language and the poetry without any explanation from me. And if *he* doesn't need it, why should anyone else, eh?

Notice, though, that he doesn't scorn to follow me along

"the sunlit paths of natural science." Indeed, he reads my books on science "with the greatest attention and respect."

I'm glad he does and I can only presume that he is grateful that I take the trouble to footnote science so that he can get a fugitive hint of its beauties.

Suppose, instead, I were to say to Mr. X, "The logarithm of two is a transcendental number; and, indeed, the logarithm of any integer to any integral base is transcendental except where the integer is equal to the base or to a power of that base."

Mr. X might then, with justification, say, "What is a transcendental number, a logarithm, and, in this case, a power and a base?"

In fact, if he were a really deep thinker, he might ask, "What is two?"

But suppose I answered then that my statement bore within it all the poetry and symmetry and beauty of mathematics ("Euclid alone has looked on beauty bare") and that to try to explain it would simply hack it up. And if Mr. X found trouble in understanding it, too bad for him. He just wasn't as bright as I was, and he could go to blazes.

But I *don't* answer that way. I explain such matters and many more, and go to a lot of trouble to do so, and then he reads those explanations with "the greatest attention and respect."

Scientists generally recognize the importance of explaining science to the nonscientist. It is interesting, then, in a rather sad way, that there exist humanists who feel themselves to be proprietors of their field, who hug literature to themselves, who mumble "the language, the poetry," and who see no reason why it should be explained to anyone as long as they themselves can continue to sniff the ambrosia.

Let us take a specific case. In the last act of *The Merchant of Venice*, Lorenzo and Jessica are enjoying an idyllic interlude at Portia's estate in Belmont, and Lorenzo says:

Sit, Jessica. Look how the floor of heaven
Is thick inlaid with patens of bright gold.
There's not the smallest orb which thou behold'st
But in his motion like an angel sings.
Still quiring to the young-eyed cherubins;
Such harmony is in immortal souls,
But whilst this muddy vesture of decay
Doth grossly close it in, we cannot hear it.

I think this passage is beautiful, for I have as keen a sense of the beauty and poetry of words as Mr. X; perhaps (is it possible?) even keener.

But what happens if someone says: "What are patens?"

After all, it is not a very common word. Does it ruin the beauty of the passage to whisper in an aside, "Small disks"?

Or what if someone asks, "What does he mean about these orbs singing like angels in their motion? What orbs? What motion? What singing?"

Am I to understand that the proper answer is, "No! Just listen to the words and the beautiful flow of language, and don't ask such philistine questions."

Does it spoil the beauty of Shakespeare's language to understand what he is saying? Or can it be that there are humanists who, qualified though they may be in esthetics, know little of the history of science, and don't know what Bill is saying and would rather not be asked.

All right, then, let's use this as a test case. I am going to explain this passage in far greater detail than I did in my book, just to show how much there is to consider in these beautiful syllables—

Anyone looking at the sky in a completely unsophisticated manner, without benefit of any astronomical training whatever, and willing to judge by appearances alone, is very likely to conclude that the Earth is covered by a smooth and flattened dome of some strong and solid material that is blue by day and black by night.

Under that solid dome is the air and the floating clouds. Above it, he may decide, is another world of gods and angels where the immortal souls of men will rise after the body dies and decays.

As a matter of fact, this is precisely the view of the early men of the Near East, for instance. On the second day of creation, says the Bible: "God said, Let there be a firmament in the midst of the waters, and let it divide the waters from the waters. And God made the firmament, and divided the waters which were under the firmament from the waters which were above the firmament" (Genesis 1:6–7).

The word "firmament" is from the Latin word *firmamentum*, which means something solid and strong. This is a translation of the Greek word *stereoma*, which means something solid and strong, and that is a translation of the original Hebrew word *raquia*, which refers to a thin metallic bowl.

In the biblical view there was water below the firmament (obviously) and water above it, too, to account for the rain. That is why in the time of Noah's flood, it is recorded that ". . . the fountains of the great deep [were] broken up, and the windows of heaven were opened" (Genesis 7:11). The expression might be accepted as metaphor, of course, but I'm sure that the unsophisticated accepted it literally.

But there's no use laughing from the height of our own painfully gained hindsight. About 700 B.C., when the material of Genesis was first being collected, the thought that the sky was a solid vault with another world above it was a reasonable conclusion to come to from the evidence available.

What's more, it would seem reasonable about 700 B.C. to suppose that the firmament stretched over but a limited portion of a flat Earth. One could see it come down and join the Earth tightly at the horizon. Few people in ancient times ever traveled far from home and the world to them was but a few miles in every direction. Even soldiers and merchants, who tramped longer distances, might feel the Earth was larger than it looked but that the world to the enlarged horizon was still flat, and still enclosed on all sides by the junction of firmament and ground. (This was also very much the medieval view and probably that of many unsophisticated moderns.)

The Greek philosophers, however, had come to the conclusion, for a number of valid reasons, that the Earth was *not* a more or less flat object of rather limited size, but a spherical object of sufficient size to dwarf the known world to small dimensions.

The firmament, then, must stretch all around the globular Earth, and to do so symmetrically, it must be another, but much larger, sphere. The apparent flattening of the firmament overhead had to be an illusion (it is!) and the Greeks spoke of what we would call the "heavenly sphere" as opposed to the "terrestrial sphere."

None of this, however, altered the concept of the firmament (or heavenly sphere) as made up of something hard and firm. What, then, were the stars?

Naturally, the first thought was that the stars were exactly what they appeared to be: tiny, glowing disks embedded in the material of the firmament ("Look how the floor of heaven is thick inlaid with patens of bright gold").

The evidence in favor of this was that the stars did not fall down, as they would surely do if they were not firmly fixed to the heavenly sphere. Secondly, the stars moved about the Earth once every twenty-four hours, with the North Star as one pivot (the other being invisible behind the southern horizon), and did so all in one piece without altering their relative positions from night to night and from year to year.

If the stars were suspended freely somewhere between

the heavenly sphere and the Earth, and for some reason did not fall, surely they would either not move at all or, if they did, would move independently. No, it made much more sense to suppose them all fixed to the heavenly sphere, and to suppose that it was the heavenly sphere that turned, carrying all the stars with itself.

But alas, this interpretation of the heavens—beautiful and austerly simple—did not account for everything.

As it happened, the Moon was clearly not imbedded in the heavenly sphere, for it did not maintain a fixed position relative to the stars. It was at a particular distance from a particular star one night, farther east the next night, still farther east the one afterward. It moved steadily west to east in such a way as to make a complete circuit of the starry sky in a little over twenty-seven days.

The Sun moved from west to east, too, relative to the stars, though much more slowly. Its motion couldn't be watched directly, of course, since no stars were visible in its neighborhood by which its position might be fixed. However, the nighttime configuration of stars shifted from night to night because, clearly, the Sun moved and blotted out slightly different portions of the sky from day to day. In that manner it could be determined that the Sun seemed to make a circuit of the sky in a little over 365 days.

If the Sun and the Moon were the only bodies to be exceptional, this might not be too bad. After all, they were very much different from the stars and could not be expected to follow the same rules.

Thus the Hebrews, in their creation myth, treated the Sun and Moon as special cases. On the fourth day of creation, "God made two great lights; the greater light to rule the day, and the lesser light to rule the night: he made the stars also" (Genesis 1:16).

It seems amusing to us today to have the stars dismissed in so offhanded a fashion, but it makes perfect sense in the light of the Hebrew knowledge of the day. The stars were all imbedded in the firmament and they served only as a background against which the motions of the Sun and the Moon could be studied.

But then it turned out that certain of the brighter stars were also anomalous in their motions and shifted positions against the background of the other stars. In fact, their motion was even stranger than that of the Moon and the Sun, for, though they moved west to east most of the time, relative to the stars, as the Moon and the Sun did, they occasionally would turn about and move east to west. Very puzzling!

The Greeks called these stars *planetes*, meaning "wanderers," as compared with the "fixed stars." The Greek word has become "planet" to us and seven of them were recognized. These included the five bright stars which we now call Mercury, Venus, Mars, Jupiter, and Saturn, and, of course, the Sun and the Moon.

What to do with them? Well, like the stars, the planets did not fall and like the stars they moved about the Earth. Therefore, like the stars, they had to be imbedded in a sphere. Since each of the seven planets moved at a different speed and in a different fashion, each had to have a separate sphere, one nested inside the other, and all nested inside the sphere of the stars.

Thus there arose the notion not of the heavenly sphere, but of the heavenly spheres, plural.

But there was only one heavenly sphere that could be seen—the blue sphere of the firmament. The fact that the other spheres were invisible was no argument, however, for their non-existence, merely for their transparency. They were sometimes called "the crystalline spheres," where the word "crystalline" was used in its older meaning as "transparent."

The Greeks then set about trying to calculate where the

different spheres were pivoted and how they must turn in order to cause each planet to move in the precise fashion in which it was observed to move. Endless complications had to be added in order to match theory with observation, but for two thousand years the complicated theory of the crystalline spheres held good, not because men of thought were perversely stupid, but because nothing else so well fit the appearances.

Even when Copernicus suggested that the Sun, not the Earth, was the center of the universe, he didn't abolish the spheres. He merely had them surrounding the Sun, with the Earth itself imbedded in one of them. It was only with Johannes Kepler—

But never mind that. The details of the motions of the crystalline spheres don't concern us in this article. Let us instead consider an apparently simpler question: In what order are the spheres nested? If we were to travel outward from Earth, which sphere would we come to first, which next, and so on.

The Greeks made the logical deduction that the closest sphere would be smallest and would therefore make a complete turn in the briefest time. Since the Moon made a complete circle against the stars in about four weeks (a far shorter time than any other planet managed to run the course), its sphere must be closest.

Arguing in this manner, the Greeks decided the next closest sphere was that of Mercury; then, in order, Venus, the Sun, Mars, Jupiter, and Saturn. And finally, of course, there was the sphere of the stars.

And how far apart were the spheres and what were their actual distances from the Earth?

That, unfortunately, was beyond the Greeks. To be sure, the Greek astronomer Hipparchus, about 150 B.C., used a perfectly valid method (after the still earlier astronomer Aristarchus) for determining the distance to the Moon, and had placed it at a distance of thirty times the Earth's diameter, which is correct, but the distance of no other heavenly body was determined with reasonable accuracy until the seventeenth century.

Now the scene switches. About 520 B.C., the Greek philosopher Pythagoras was plucking strings, and found that he could evoke notes that harmonized well together if he used strings whose lengths were simply related. One string might be twice the length of another; or three strings might have lengths that were in the ration of 3:4:5.

The details are irrelevant, but to Pythagoras it seemed highly significant that there should be a connection between pleasing sounds and small whole numbers. It fit in with his rather mystical notion that everything in the universe was related to simple ratios and numbers.

Those who followed in his footsteps after his death accentuated the mysticism and it seemed to the Pythagoreans that they now had a way of deciding not only the how of planets, but the why as well. Since numbers governed the universe, one ought to be able to deduce the way in which the universe ought to be constructed.

For instance, 10 was a particularly impressive number. (Why? Well, for one thing, 1 + 2 + 3 + 4 = 10, and this seems to have some mystical value.) In order, then, for the universe to function well, it had to be composed of ten spheres.

Of course, there were only eight spheres, one for the stars and one for each of the seven planets, but that didn't stop the Pythagoreans. They decided that the Earth moved around some central fire of which the Sun was only a reflection, and worked up a reason for explaining why the central fire was invisible. That added a ninth sphere for the Earth. In addition, they imagined another planet on the opposite side of the central fire, a "counter-Earth". The counter-Earth kept pace with the Earth and stayed always beyond the central fire and was thus never seen. It's sphere was the tenth.

In addition, the Pythagoreans thought that the spheres were nested inside each other in such a way that their distances of separation bore simple ratios to one another and produced harmonious notes in their motion as a result (like the plucking of strings of simply related lengths). Originally, I imagine, the Pythagoreans may have advanced this notion of harmonious notes only as a metaphor to represent the simply related distances, but later mystics accepted the notes as literally existent. They became "the music of the spheres."

Of course, no one ever heard any music from the sky, so it had to be assumed to be inaudible to men on Earth. It is this notion that causes Shakespeare to speak of an orb that "in his motion like an angel sings" but with sounds that can be heard only in heaven ("Such harmony is in immortal souls"). While men's souls are still draped in their earthly bodies, they are deaf to it ("whilst this muddy vesture of decay doth grossly close it in, we cannot hear it").

Well, then, does understanding Lorenzo's speech in terms of ancient astronomy spoil its beauty? Does it not seem that to understand him adds to the interest? Does it not remove the nagging question of "But what does it mean?" that otherwise distracts from an appreciation of the passage?

It may be, of course, that Mr. X is the kind who never asks "But what does it mean?" It may be that for him understanding is irrelevant. If so, he and I are not soul mates. It may even be that Mr. X is the kind of obscurantist who finds that understanding decreases beauty. If so, he and I are even less soul mates.

And yet, let me point out that there is something in this very passage that could be of interest to Shakespearian scholars *if* they thoroughly understood what Shakespeare was talking about.

As almost everyone knows, there are many who feel that Shakespeare did not write the plays attributed to him. They feel that someone else did, with the person most frequently credited being Francis Bacon, who was an almost exact contemporary of Shakespeare.

The argument very often heard is that Shakespeare was just a fellow from the provinces with very little education and that he could not possibly have written so profoundly learned a set of plays. Bacon, on the other hand, was a great philosopher and one of the most intensely educated people of his time. Bacon, therefore, could easily have written the plays.

Shakespearian scholars, when they argue the matter at all, are forced to maintain that Shakespeare was much better educated than he is given credit for being and that therefore he was learned enough to write his plays. Since virtually nothing is known of Shakespeare's life, the argument will never be settled in that fashion.

Why not turn matters around, then, and argue that Bacon was *too* educated to write Shakespeare's plays, that there exist errors in the plays that Bacon could never possibly have made and that would just suit an insufficiently educated fellow from the sticks?

Consider Lorenzo's speech. Lorenzo is talking about the *stars*; these are the "patens of bright gold" with which "the floor of heaven is thick inlaid." Lorenzo (hence Shakespeare) seems to think that each star has a separate sphere and that each gives out its own note ("There's not the smallest orb which thou behold'st/But in his motion like an angel sings").

Lest you think I'm misinterpreting the speech, let's take a clearer case.

In Act II of *A Midsummer Night's Dream*, Oberon is

reminding Puck of a time they listened to a mermaid who sang with such supernal beauty that

> . . . the rude sea grew civil at her song,
> And certain stars shot madly from their spheres,
> To hear the sea maid's music.

The use of the plural "spheres" shows again that Shakespeare thinks that each star has its separate sphere.

This is wrong. There is a sphere for each planet; one for the Earth itself, if you like; one for the counter-Earth; one for any imaginary planet you wish. However, all the ancient theories agreed that the "fixed stars" were all imbedded in a single sphere.

To imagine separate spheres for each star, as Shakespeare does more than once in his plays, is to display a lack of knowledge of Greek astronomy. This is a lack of knowledge that Francis Bacon could not possibly have displayed; hence we might fairly argue that Francis Bacon could not possibly have written Shakespeare's plays.

Well, don't get me wrong. I don't want to imply that I received only bad reviews for my *Guide to Shakespeare*. Actually, most of the reviews were quite complimentary and were an entire pleasure to read.

Just the same, I had better start preparing myself for the occasional review by the "outraged specialist" type that I will surely get when *Asimov's Annotated "Don Juan"* is published.

MIRROR IMAGE

The Three Laws of Robotics

1: A robot may not injure a human being or, through inaction, allow a human being to come to harm.
2: A robot must obey the orders given it by human beings except where such orders would conflict with the First Law.
3: A robot must protect its own existence as long as such protection does not conflict with the First or Second Law.

Lije Baley had just decided to relight his pipe, when the door of his office opened without a preliminary knock, or announcement, of any kind. Baley looked up in pronounced annoyance and then dropped his pipe. It said a good deal for the state of his mind that he left it lie where it had fallen.

"R. Daneel Olivaw," he said, in a kind of mystified excitement. "Jehoshaphat! It *is* you, isn't it?"

"You are quite right," said the tall, bronzed newcomer, his even features never flickering for a moment out of their accustomed calm. "I regret surprising you by entering without warning, but the situation is a delicate one and there must be as little involvement as possible on the part of the men and robots even in this place. I am, in any case, pleased to see you again, friend Elijah."

And the robot held out his right hand in a gesture as thoroughly human as was his appearance. It was Baley who was so unmanned by his astonishment as to stare at the hand with a momentary lack of understanding.

But then he seized it in both his, feeling its warm

firmness. "But Daneel, *why*? You're welcome any time, but—What is this situation that is a delicate one? Are we in trouble again? Earth, I mean?"

"No, friend Elijah, it does not concern Earth. The situation to which I refer as a delicate one is, to outward appearances, a small thing. A dispute between mathematicians, nothing more. As we happened, quite by accident, to be within any easy Jump of Earth—"

"This dispute took place on a starship, then?"

"Yes, indeed. A small dispute, yet to the humans involved astonishingly large."

Baley could not help but smile. "I'm not surprised you find humans astonishing. They do not obey the Three Laws."

"That is, indeed, a shortcoming," said R. Daneel, gravely, "and I think humans themselves are puzzled by humans. It may be that you are less puzzled than are the men of other worlds because so many more human beings live on Earth than on the Spacer worlds. If so, and I believe it is so, you could help us."

R. Daneel paused momentarily and then said, perhaps a shade too quickly, "And yet there are rules of human behavior which I have learned. It would seem, for instance, that I am deficient in etiquette, by human standards, not to have asked after your wife and child."

"They are doing well. The boy is in college and Jessie is involved in local politics. The amenities are taken care of. Now tell me how you come to be here."

"As I said, we were within an easy Jump of Earth," said R. Daneel, "so I suggested to the captain that we consult you."

"And the captain agreed?" Baley had a sudden picture of the proud and autocratic captain of a Spacer starship consenting to make a landing on Earth—of all worlds—and to consult an Earthman—of all people.

"I believe," said R. Daneel, "that he was in a position where he would have agreed to anything. In addition, I praised you very highly; although, to be sure, I stated only the truth. Finally, I agreed to conduct all negotiations so that none of the crew, or passengers, would need to enter any of the Earthman cities."

"And talk to any Earthman, yes. But what has happened?"

"The passengers of the starship, *Eta Carina*, included two mathematicians who were traveling to Aurora to attend an interstellar conference on neurobiophysics. It is about these mathematicians, Alfred Barr Humboldt and Gennao Sabbat, that the dispute centers. Have you perhaps, friend Elijah, heard of one, or both, of them?"

"Neither one," said Baley, firmly. "I know nothing about mathematics. Look, Daneel, surely you haven't told anyone I'm a mathematics buff or—"

"Not at all, friend Elijah. I know you are not. Nor does it matter, since the exact nature of the mathematics involved is in no way relevant to the point of issue."

"Well, then, go on."

"Since you do not know either man, friend Elijah, let me tell you that Dr. Humboldt is well into his twenty-seventh decade—pardon me, friend Elijah?"

"Nothing. Nothing," said Baley, irritably. He had merely muttered to himself, more or less incoherently, in a natural reaction to the extended life-spans of the Spacers. "And he's still active, despite his age? On Earth, mathematicians after thirty or so . . ."

Daneel said, calmly, "Dr. Humboldt is one of the top three mathematicians, by long-established repute, in the galaxy. Certainly he is still active. Dr. Sabbat, on the other hand, is quite young, not yet fifty, but he has already established himself as the most remarkable new talent in the most abstruse branches of mathematics."

"They're both great, then," said Baley. He remembered his pipe and picked it up. He decided there was no point in lighting it now and knocked out the dottle. "What happened? Is this a murder case? Did one of them apparently kill the other?"

"Of course two men of great reputation, one is trying to destroy that of the other. By human values, I believe this may be regarded as worse than physical murder."

"Sometimes, I suppose. Which one is trying to destroy the other?"

"Why, that, friend Elijah, is precisely the point of issue. Which?"

"Go on."

"Dr. Humboldt tells the story clearly. Shortly before he boarded the starship, he had an insight into a possible method of analyzing neural pathways from changes in microwave absorption patterns of local cortical areas. The insight was a purely mathematical technique of extraordinary subtlety, but I cannot, of course, either understand or sensibly transmit the details. These do not, however, matter. Dr. Humboldt considered the matter and was more convinced each hour that he had something revolutionary on hand, something that would dwarf all his previous accomplishments in mathematics. Then he discovered that Dr. Sabbat was on board."

"Ah. And he tried it out on young Sabbat?"

"Exactly. The two had met at professional meetings before and knew each other thoroughly by reputation. Humboldt went into it with Sabbat in great detail. Sabbat backed Humboldt's analysis completely and was unstinting in his praise of the importance of the discovery and of the ingenuity of the discoverer. Heartened and reassured by this, Humboldt prepared a paper outlining, in summary, his work and, two days later, prepared to have it forwarded subetherically to the co-chairmen of the conference at Aurora, in order that he might officially establish his priority and arrange for possible discussion before the sessions were closed. To his surprise, he found that Sabbat was ready with a paper of his own, essentially the same as Humboldt's, and Sabbat was also preparing to have it subetherized to Aurora."

"I suppose Humboldt was furious."

"Quite!"

"And Sabbat? What was his story?"

"Precisely the same as Humboldt's. Word for word."

"Then just what is the problem?"

"Except for the mirror-image exchange of names. According to Sabbat, it was he who had the insight, and he who consulted Humboldt; it was Humboldt who agreed with the analysis and praised it."

"Then each one claims the idea is his and that the other stole it. It doesn't sound like a problem to me at all. In matters of scholarship, it would seem only necessary to produce the records of research, dated and initialed. Judgment as to priority can be made from that. Even if one is falsified, that might be discovered through internal inconsistencies."

"Ordinarily, friend Elijah, you would be right, but this is mathematics, and not an experimental science. Dr. Humboldt claims to have worked out the essentials in his head. Nothing was put in writing until the paper itself was prepared. Dr. Sabbat, of course, says precisely the same."

"Well, then, be more drastic and get it over with, for sure. Subject each one to a psychic probe and find out which of the two is lying."

R. Daneel shook his head slowly. "Friend Elijah, you do not understand these men. They are both of rank and scholarship, Fellows of the Imperial Academy. As such, they cannot be subjected to trial of professional conduct except by a jury of their peers—their professional peers—unless they personally and voluntarily waive that right."

"Put it to them, then. The guilty man won't waive the right because he can't afford to face the psychic probe. The innocent man will waive it at once. You won't even have to use the probe."

"It does not work that way, friend Elijah. To waive the right in such a case—to be investigated by laymen—is a serious and perhaps irrecoverable blow to prestige. Both men steadfastly refuse to waive the right to special trial, as a matter of pride. The question of guilt, or innocence, is quite subsidiary."

"In that case, let it go for now. Put the matter in cold storage until you get to Aurora. At the neurobiophysical conference, there will be a huge supply of professional peers, and then—"

"That would mean a tremendous blow to science itself, friend Elijah. Both men would suffer for having been the instrument of scandal. Even the innocent one would be blamed for having been party to a situation so distasteful. It would be felt that it should have been settled quietly out of court at all costs."

"All right. I'm not a Spacer, but I'll try to imagine that this attitude makes sense. What do the men in question say?"

"Humboldt agrees thoroughly. He says that if Sabbat will admit theft of the idea and allow Humboldt to proceed with transmission of the paper—or at least its delivery at the conference, he will not press charges. Sabbat's misdeed will remain secret with him; and, of course, with the captain, who is the only other human to be party to the dispute."

"But young Sabbat will not agree?"

"On the contrary, he agreed with Dr. Humboldt to the last detail—with the reversal of names. Still the mirror-image."

"So they just sit there, stalemated?"

"Each, I believe, friend Elijah, is waiting for the other to give in and admit guilt."

"Well, then, wait."

"The captain has decided this cannot be done. There are two alternatives to waiting, you see. The first is that both will remain stubborn so that when the starship lands on Aurora, the intellectual scandal will break. The captain, who is responsible for justice on board ship, will suffer disgrace for not having been able to settle the matter quietly and that, to him, is quite insupportable."

"And the second alternative?"

"Is that one, or the other, of the mathematicians will indeed admit to wrongdoing. But will the one who confesses do so out of actual guilt, or out of noble desire to prevent the scandal? Would it be right to deprive of credit one who is sufficiently ethical to prefer to lose that credit than to see science as a whole suffer? Or else, the guilty party will confess at the last moment, and in such a way as to make it appear he does so only for the sake of science, thus escaping the disgrace of his deed and casting its shadow upon the other. The captain will be the only man to know all this but he does not wish to spend the rest of his life wondering whether he has been a party to a grotesque miscarriage of justice."

Baley sighed. "A game of intellectual chicken. Who'll break first as Aurora comes nearer and nearer? Is that the whole story now, Daneel?"

"Not quite. There are witnesses to the transaction."

"Jehoshaphat! Why didn't you say so at once. *What* witnesses?"

"Dr. Humboldt's personal servant—"

"A robot, I suppose."

"Yes, certainly. He is called R. Preston. This servant, R.

Preston, was present during the initial conference and he bears out Dr. Humboldt in every detail."

"You mean he says that the idea was Dr. Humboldt's to begin with; that Dr. Humboldt detailed it to Dr. Sabbat; that Dr. Sabbat praised the idea, and so on."

"Yes, in full detail."

"I see. Does that settle the matter or not? Presumably not."

"You are quite right. It does not settle the matter, for there is a second witness. Dr. Sabbat also has a personal servant, R. Idda, another robot of, as it happens, the same model as R. Preston, made, I believe, in the same year in the same factory. Both have been in service for an equal period of time."

"An odd coincidence—very odd."

"A fact, I am afraid, and it makes it difficult to arrive at any judgment based on obvious differences between the two servants."

"R. Idda, then, tells the same story as R. Preston?"

"Precisely the same story, except for the mirror-image reversal of the names."

"R. Idda stated, then, that young Sabbat, the one not yet fifty"—Lije Baley did not entirely keep the sardonic note out of his voice; he himself was not yet fifty and he felt far from young—"had the idea to begin with; that he detailed it to Dr. Humboldt, who was loud in his praises, and so on."

"Yes, friend Elijah."

"And one robot is lying, then."

"So it would seem."

"It should be easy to tell which. I imagine even a superficial examination by a good roboticist—"

"A roboticist is not enough in this case, friend Elijah. Only a qualified robopsychologist would carry weight enough and experience enough to make a decision in a case of this importance. There is no one so qualified on board ship. Such an examination can be performed only when we reach Aurora—"

"And by then the crud hits the fan. Well, you're here on Earth. We can scare up a robopsychologist, and surely anything that happens on Earth will never reach the ears of Aurora and there will be no scandal."

"Except that neither Dr. Humboldt, nor Dr. Sabbat, will allow his servants to be investigated by a robopsychologist of Earth. The Earthman would have to—" He paused.

Lije Baley said stolidly, "He'd have to touch the robot."

"These are old servants, well thought of—"

"And not to be sullied by the touch of Earthmen. Then what do you want me to do, damn it?" He paused, grimacing. "I'm sorry, R. Daneel, but I see no reason for your having involved me."

"I was on the ship on a mission utterly irrelevant to the problem at hand. The captain turned to me because he had to turn to someone. I seemed human enough to talk to, and robot enough to be a safe recipient of confidences. He told me the whole story and asked what I would do. I realized the next Jump could take us as easily to Earth as to our target. I told the captain that, although I was at as much a loss to resolve the mirror-image as he was, there was on Earth one who might help."

"Jehoshaphat!" muttered Baley under his breath.

"Consider, friend Elijah, that if you succeed in solving this puzzle, it would do your career good and Earth itself might benefit. The matter could not be publicized, of course, but the captain is a man of some influence on his home world and he would be grateful."

"You just put a greater strain on me."

"I have every confidence," said R. Daneel, stolidly, "that you already have some idea as to what procedure ought to be followed."

"Do you? I suppose that the obvious procedure is to interview the two mathematicians, one of whom would seem to be a thief."

"I'm afraid, friend Elijah, that neither one will come into the city. Nor would either one be willing to have you come to them."

"And there is no way of forcing a Spacer to allow contact with an Earthman, no matter what the emergency. Yes, I understand that, Daneel—but I was thinking of an interview by closed-circuit television."

"Nor that. They will not submit to interrogation by an Earthman."

"Then what do they want of me? Could I speak to the robots?"

"They would not allow the robots to come here, either."

"Jehoshaphat, Daneel. *You've* come."

"That was my own decision. I have permission, while on board ship, to make decisions of that sort without veto by any human being but the captain himself—and he was eager to establish the contact. I, having known you, decided that television contact was insufficient. I wished to shake your hand."

Lije Baley softened. "I appreciate that, Daneel, but I still honestly wish you could have refrained from thinking of me at all in this case. Can I talk to the robots by television at least?"

"That, I think, can be arranged."

"Something, at least. That means I would be doing the work of a robopsychologist—in a crude sort of way."

"But you are a detective, friend Elijah, not a robopsychologist."

"Well, let it pass. Now before I see them, let's think a bit. Tell me: is it possible that both robots are telling the truth? Perhaps the conversation between the two mathematicians was equivocal. Perhaps it was of such a nature that each robot could honestly believe its own master was proprietor of the idea. Or perhaps one robot heard only one portion of the discussion and the other another portion, so that each could suppose its own master was proprietor of the idea."

"That is quite impossible, friend Elijah. Both robots repeat the conversation in identical fashion. And the two repetitions are fundamentally inconsistent."

"Then it is absolutely certain that one of the robots is lying?"

"Yes."

"Will I be able to see the transcript of all evidence given so far in the presence of the captain, if I should want to?"

"I thought you would ask that and I have copies with me."

"Another blessing. Have the robots been cross-examined at all, and is that cross-examination included in the transcript?"

"The robots have merely repeated their tales. Cross-examination would be conducted only by robopsychologists."

"Or by myself?"

"You are a detective, friend Elijah, not a—"

"All right, R. Daneel. I'll try to get the Spacer psychology straight. A detective can do it because he isn't a robopsychologist. Let's think further. Ordinarily a robot will not lie, but he will do so if necessary to maintain the Three Laws. He might lie to protect, in legitimate fashion, his own existence in accordance with the Third Law. He is more apt to lie if that is necessary to follow a legitimate order given him by a human being in accordance with the Second Law. He is most apt to lie if that is necessary to save a human life, or to prevent harm from coming to a human in accordance with the First Law."

"Yes."

"And in this case, each robot would be defending the

professional reputation of his master, and would lie if it were necessary to do so. Under the circumstances, the professional reputation would be nearly equivalent to life and there might be a near-First-Law urgency to the lie."

"Yet by the lie, each servant would be harming the professional reputation of the other's master, friend Elijah."

"So it would, but each robot might have a clearer conception of the value of its own master's reputation and honestly judge it to be greater than that of the other's. The lesser harm would be done by his lie, he would suppose, than by the truth."

Having said that, Lije Baley remained quiet for a moment. Then he said, "All right, then, can you arrange to have me talk to one of the robots—to R. Idda first, I think?"

"Dr. Sabbat's robot?"

"Yes," said Baley, dryly, "the young fellow's robot."

"It will take me but a few minutes," said R. Daneel. "I have a micro-receiver outfitted with a projector. I will need merely a blank wall and I think this one will do if you will allow me to move some of these film cabinets."

"Go ahead. Will I have to talk into a microphone of some sort?"

"No, you will be able to talk in an ordinary manner. Please pardon me, friend Elijah, for a moment of further delay. I will have to contact the ship and arrange for R. Idda to be interviewed."

"If that will take some time, Daneel, how about giving me the transcripted material of the evidence so far."

Lije Baley lit his pipe while R. Daneel set up the equipment, and leafed through the flimsy sheets he had been handed.

The minutes passed and R. Daneel said, "If you are ready, friend Elijah, R. Idda is. Or would you prefer a few more minutes with the transcript?"

"No," sighed Baley, "I'm not learning anything new. Put him on and arrange to have the interview recorded and transcribed."

R. Idda, unreal in two-dimensional projection against the wall, was basically metallic in structure—not at all the humanoid creature that R. Daneel was. His body was tall but blocky, and there was very little to distinguish him from the robots Baley had seen, except for minor structural details.

Baley said, "Greetings, R. Idda."

"Greetings, sir," said R. Idda, in a mutted voice that sounded surprisingly humanoid.

"You are the personal servant of Gennao Sabbat, are you not?"

"I am sir."

"For how long, boy?"

"For twenty-two years, sir."

"And your master's reputation is valuable to you?"

"Yes, sir."

"Would you consider it of importance to protect that reputation?"

"Yes, sir."

"As important to protect his reputation as his physical life?"

"No, sir."

"As important to protect his reputation as the reputation of another?"

R. Idda hesitated. He said, "Such cases must be decided on their individual merit, sir. There is no way of establishing a general rule."

Baley hesitated. These Spacer robots spoke more smoothly and intellectually than Earth-models did. He was not at all sure he could outthink one.

He said, "If you decided that the reputation of your

master were more important than that of another, say, that of Alfred Barr Humboldt, would you lie to protect your master's reputation?"

"I would, sir."

"Did you lie in your testimony concerning your master in his controversy with Dr. Humboldt?"

"No, sir."

"But if you were lying, you would deny you were lying in order to protect that lie, wouldn't you?"

"Yes, sir."

"Well, then," said Baley, "let's consider this. Your master, Gennao Sabbat, is a young man of great reputation in mathematics, but he is a young man. If, in this controversy with Dr. Humboldt, he had succumbed to temptation and had acted unethically, he would suffer a certain eclipse of reputation, but he is young and would have ample time to recover. He would have many intellectual triumphs ahead of him and men would eventually look upon this plagiaristic attempt as the mistake of a hot-blooded youth, deficient in judgment. It would be something that would be made up for in the future.

"If, on the other hand, it were Dr. Humboldt who succumbed to temptation, the matter would be much more serious. He is an old man whose great deeds have spread over centuries. His reputation has been unblemished hitherto. All of that, however, would be forgotten in the light of this one crime of his later years, and he would have no opportunity to make up for it in the comparatively short time remaining to him. There would be little more that he could accomplish. There would be so many more years of work ruined in Humboldt's case than in that of your master and so much less opportunity to win back his position. You see, don't you, that Humboldt faces the worse situation and deserves the greater consideration?"

There was a long pause. Then R. Idda said, with

unmoved voice, "My evidence was a lie. It was Dr. Humboldt whose work it was, and my master has attempted, wrongfully, to appropriate the credit."

Baley said, "Very well, boy. You are instructed to say nothing to anyone about this until given permission by the captain of the ship. You are excused."

The screen blanked out and Baley puffed at his pipe. "Do you suppose the captain heard that, Daneel?"

"I am sure of it. He is the only witness, except for us."

"Good. Now for the other."

"But is there any point to that, friend Elijah, in view of what R. Idda has confessed?"

"Of course there is. R. Idda's confession means nothing."

"Nothing?"

"Nothing at all. I pointed out that Dr. Humboldt's position was the worse. Naturally, if he were lying to protect Sabbat, he would switch to the truth as, in fact, he claimed to have done. On the other hand, if he were telling the truth, he would switch to a lie to protect Humboldt. It's still mirror-image and we haven't gained anything."

"But then what will we gain by questioning R. Preston?"

"Nothing, if the mirror-image were perfect—but it is not. After all, one of the robots *is* telling the truth to begin with, and one *is* lying to begin with, and that is a point of asymmetry. Let me see R. Preston. And if the transcription of R. Idda's examination is done, let me have it."

The projector came into use again. R. Preston stared out of it; identical with R. Idda in every respect, except for some trivial chest design.

Baley said, "Greetings, R. Preston." He kept the record of R. Idda's examination before him as he spoke.

"Greetings, sir," said R. Preston. His voice was identical with that of R. Idda.

"You are the personal servant of Alfred Barr Humboldt, are you not?"

"I am, sir."

"For how long, boy?"

"For twenty-two years, sir."

"And your master's reputation is valuable to you?"

"Yes, sir."

"Would you consider it of importance to protect that reputation?"

"Yes, sir."

"As important to protect his reputation as his physical life?"

"No, sir."

"As important to protect his reputation as the reputation of another?"

R. Preston hesitated. He said, "Such cases must be decided on their individual merit, sir. There is no way of establishing a general rule."

Baley said, "If you decided that the reputation of your master were more important than that of another, say, that of Gennao Sabbat, would you lie to protect your master's reputation?"

"I would, sir."

"Did you lie in your testimony concerning your master in his controversy with Dr. Sabbat?"

"No, sir."

"But if you were lying, you would deny you were lying, in order to protect that lie, wouldn't you?"

"Yes, sir."

"Well, then," said Baley, "let's consider this. Your master, Alfred Barr Humboldt, is an old man of great reputation in mathematics, but he is an old man. If, in this controversy with Dr. Sabbat, he had succumbed to temptation and had acted unethically, he would suffer a certain eclipse of reputation, but his great age and his centuries of accomplishments would stand against that and would win out. Men would look upon this plagiaristic attempt as the mistake of a perhaps-sick old man, no longer certain in judgment.

"If, on the other hand, it were Dr. Sabbat who had succumbed to temptation, the matter would be much more serious. He is a young man, with a far less secure reputation. He would ordinarily have centuries ahead of him in which he might accumulate knowledge and achieve great things. This will be closed to him, now, obscured by one mistake of his youth. He has a much longer future to lose than your master has. You see, don't you, that Sabbat faces the worse situation and deserves the greater consideration?"

There was a long pause. Then R. Preston said, with unmoved voice, "My evidence was as I—"

At that point, he broke off and said nothing more.

Baley said, "Please continue, R. Preston."

There was no response.

R. Daneel said, "I am afraid, friend Elijah, that R. Preston is in stasis. He is out of commission."

"Well, then," said Baley, "we have finally produced an asymmetry. From this, we can see who the guilty person is."

"In what way, friend Elijah?"

"Think it out. Suppose you were a person who had committed no crime and that your personal robot were a witness to that. There would be nothing you need to do. Your robot would tell the truth and bear you out. If, however, you were a person who *had* committed the crime, you would have to depend on your robot to lie. That would be a somewhat riskier position, for although the robot would lie, if necessary, the greater inclination would be to tell the truth, so that the lie would be less firm than the truth would be. To prevent that, the crime-committing person would very likely have to *order* the robot to lie. In this way.

First Law would be strengthened by Second Law; perhaps very substantially strengthened."

"That would seem reasonable," said R. Daneel.

"Suppose we have one robot of each type. One robot would switch from truth, unreinforced, to the lie, and could do so after some hesitation, without serious trouble. The other robot would switch from the lie, *strongly reinforced*, to the truth, but could do so only at the risk of burning out various positronic-track-ways in his brain and falling into stasis."

"And since R. Preston went into stasis—"

"R. Preston's master, Dr. Humboldt, is the man guilty of plagiarism. If you transmit this to the captain and urge him to face Dr. Humboldt with the matter at once, he may force a confession. If so, I hope you will tell me immediately."

"I will certainly do so. You will excuse me, friend Elijah? I must talk to the captain privately."

"Certainly. Use the conference room. It is shielded."

Baley could do no work of any kind in R. Daneel's absence. He sat in uneasy silence. A great deal would depend on the value of his analysis, and he was acutely aware of his lack of expertise in robotics.

R. Daneel was back in half an hour—very nearly the longest half hour of Baley's life.

There was no use, of course, in trying to determine what had happened from the expression of the humanoid's impassive face. Baley tried to keep his face impassive.

"Yes, R. Daneel?" he asked.

"Precisely as you said, friend Elijah. Dr. Humboldt has confessed. He was counting, he said, on Dr. Sabbat giving way and allowing Dr. Humboldt to have this one last triumph. The crisis is over and you will find the captain grateful. He has given me permission to tell you that he admires your subtlety greatly and I believe that I, myself, will achieve favor for having suggested you."

"Good," said Baley, his knees weak and his forehead moist now that his decision had proven correct, "but Jehosphaphat, R. Daneel, don't put me on the spot like that again, will you?"

"I will try not to, friend Elijah. All will depend, of course, on the importance of a crisis, on your nearness, and on certain other factors. Meanwhile, I have a question—"

"Yes?"

"Was it not possible to suppose that passage from a lie to the truth was easy, while passage from the truth to a lie was difficult? And in that case, would not the robot in stasis have been going from a truth to a lie, and since R. Preston was in stasis, might one not have drawn the conclusion that it was Dr. Humboldt who was innocent and Dr. Sabbat who was guilty?"

"Yes, R. Daneel. It was possible to argue that way, but it was the other argument that proved it. Humboldt did confess, didn't he?"

"He did. But with arguments possible in both directions, how could you, friend Elijah, so quickly pick the correct one?"

For a moment, Baley's lips twitched. Then he relaxed and they curved into a smile. "Because, R. Daneel, I took into account human reactions, not robotic ones. I know more about human beings than about robots. In other words, I had an idea as to which mathematician was guilty before I ever interviewed the robots. Once I provoked an asymmetric response in them, I simply interpreted it in such a way as to place the guilt on the one I already believed to be guilty. The robotic response was dramatic enough to break down the guilty man; my own analysis of human behavior might not have been sufficient to do so."

"I am curious to know what your analysis of human behavior was?"

"Jehoshaphat, R. Daneel; think, and you won't have to ask. There is another point of asymmetry in this tale of mirror-image besides the matter of true-and-false. There is the matter of the age of the two mathematicians; one is quite old and one is quite young."

"Yes, of course, but what then?"

"Why, this. I can see a young man, flushed with a sudden, startling and revolutionary idea, consulting in the matter an old man whom he has, from his early student days, thought of as a demigod in the field. I can *not* see an old man, rich in honors and used to triumphs, coming up with a sudden, startling and revolutionary idea, consulting a man centuries his junior whom he is bound to think of as a young whippersnapper—or whatever term a Spacer would use. Then, too, if a young man had the chance, would he try to steal the idea of a revered demigod? It would be unthinkable. On the other hand, an old man, conscious of declining powers, might well snatch at one last chance of fame and consider a baby in the field to have no rights he was bound to observe. In short, it was not conceivable that Sabbat steal Humboldt's idea; and from both angles, Dr. Humboldt was guilty."

R. Daneel considered that for a long time. Then he held out his hand. "I must leave now, friend Elijah. It was good to see you. May we meet again soon."

Baley gripped the robot's hand, warmly, "If you don't mind, R. Daneel," he said "not too soon."

LIGHT VERSE

The very last person anyone would expect to be a murderer was Mrs. Avis Lardner. Widow of the great astronaut-martyr, she was a philanthropist, an art collector, a hostess extraordinary, and, everyone agreed, an artistic genius. But above all, she was the gentlest and kindest human being one could imagine.

Her husband, William J. Lardner, died, as we all know, of the effects of radiation from a solar flare, after he had deliberately remained in space so that a passenger vessel might make it safely to Space Station 5.

Mrs. Lardner had received a generous pension for that, and she had then invested wisely and well. By late middle age she was very wealthy.

Her house was a showplace, a veritable museum, containing a small but extremely select collection of extraordinarily beautiful jeweled objects. From a dozen different cultures she had obtained relics of almost every conceivable artifact that could be embedded with jewels and made to serve the aristocracy of that culture. She had one of the first jeweled wristwatches manufactured in America, a jeweled dagger from Cambodia, a jeweled pair of spectacles from Italy, and so on almost endlessly.

All was open for inspection. The artifacts were not insured, and there were no ordinary security provisions. There was no need for anything conventional, for Mrs. Lardner maintained a large staff of robot servants, all of whom could be relied on to guard every item with imperturbable concentration, irreproachable honesty, and irrevocable efficiency.

Everyone knew the existence of those robots and there is no record of any attempt at theft, ever.

And then, of course, there was her light-sculpture. How Mrs. Lardner discovered her own genius at the art, no guest at her many lavish entertainments could guess. On each occasion, however, when her house was thrown open to guests, a new symphony of light shone throughout the rooms; three-dimensional curves and solids in melting color, some pure and some fusing in startling, crystalline effects that bathed every guest in wonder and somehow always adjusted itself so as to make Mrs. Lardner's blue-white hair and soft, unlined face gently beautiful.

It was for the light-sculpture more than anything else that the guests came. It was never the same twice, and never failed to explore new experimental avenues of art. Many people who could afford light-consoles prepared light-sculptures for amusement, but no one could approach Mrs. Lardner's expertise. Not even those who considered themselves professional artists.

She herself was charmingly modest about it. "No, no," she would protest when someone waxed lyrical. "I wouldn't call it 'poetry in light.' That's far too kind. At most, I would say it was mere 'light verse.' " And everyone smiled at her gentle wit.

Though she was often asked, she would never create

light-sculpture for any occasion but her own parties. "That would be commercialization," she said.

She had no objection, however, to the preparation of elaborate holograms of her sculptures so that they might be made permanent and reproduced in museums of art all over the world. Nor was there ever a charge for any use that might be made of her light-sculptures.

"I couldn't ask a penny," she said, spreading her arms wide. "It's free to all. After all, I have no further use for it myself." It was true! She never used the same light-sculpture twice.

When the holograms were taken, she was cooperation itself. Watching benignly at every step, she was always ready to order her robot servants to help. "Please, Courtney," she would say, "would you be so kind as to adjust the step ladder?"

It was her fashion. She always addressed her robots with the most formal courtesy.

Once, years before, she had been almost scolded by a government functionary from the Bureau of Robots and Mechanical Men. "You can't do that," he said severely. "It interferes with their efficiency. They are constructed to follow orders, and the more clearly you give those orders, the more efficiently they follow them. When you ask with elaborate politeness, it is difficult for them to understand that an order is being given. They react more slowly."

Mrs. Lardner lifted her aristocratic head. "I do not ask for speed and efficiency," she said. "I ask goodwill. My robots love me."

The government functionary might have explained that robots cannot love, but he withered under her hurt but gentle glance.

It was notorious that Mrs. Lardner never even returned a robot to the factory for adjustment. Their positronic brains are enormously complex, and once in ten times or so the adjustment is not perfect as it leaves the factory. Sometimes the error does not show up for a period of time, but whenever it does, U.S. Robots and Mechanical Men Corporation always makes the adjustment free of charge.

Mrs. Lardner shook her head. "Once a robot is in my house," she said, "and has performed his duties, any minor eccentricities must be borne with. I will not have him manhandled."

It was the worse thing possible to try to explain that a robot was but a machine. She would say very stiffly, "Nothing that is as intelligent as a robot can ever be *but* a machine. I treat them as people."

And that was that!

She kept even Max, although he was almost helpless. He could scarcely understand what was expected of him. Mrs. Lardner denied that strenuously, however. "Not at all," she would say firmly. "He can take hats and coats and store them very well, indeed. He can hold objects for me. He can do many things."

"But why not have him adjusted?" asked a friend, once.

"Oh, I couldn't. He's himself. He's very lovable, you know. After all, a positronic brain is so complex that no one can ever tell in just what way it's off. If he were made perfectly normal there would be no way to adjust him back to the lovability he now has. I won't give that up."

"But if he's maladjusted," said the friend, looking at Max nervously, "might he not be dangerous?"

"Never," laughed Mrs. Lardner. "I've had him for years. He's completely harmless and quite a dear."

Actually he looked like all the other robots, smooth, metallic, vaguely human but expressionless.

To the gentle Mrs. Lardner, however, they were all individual, all sweet, all lovable. It was the kind of woman she was.

How could she commit murder?

• • •

The very last person anyone would expect to be murdered would be John Semper Travis. Introverted and gentle, he was in the world but not of it. He had that peculiar mathematical turn of mind that made it possible for him to work out in his mind the complicated tapestry of the myriad positronic brain-paths in a robot's mind.

He was chief engineer of U.S. Robots and Mechanical Men Corporation.

But he was also an enthusiastic amateur in light-sculpture. He had written a book on the subject, trying to show that the type of mathematics he used in working out positronic brain-paths might be modified into a guide to the production of aesthetic light-sculpture.

His attempt at putting theory into practice was a dismal failure, however. The sculptures he himself, produced, following his mathematical principles, were stodgy, mechanical, and uninteresting.

It was the only reason for unhappiness in his quiet, introverted, and secure life, and yet it was reason enough for him to be very unhappy indeed. He *knew* his theories were right, yet he could not make them work. If he could but produce *one* great piece of light-sculpture—

Naturally, he knew of Mrs. Lardner's light-sculpture. She was universally hailed as a genius, yet Travis knew she could not understand even the simplest aspect of robotic mathematics. He had corresponded with her but she consistently refused to explain her methods, and he wondered if she had any at all. Might it not be mere intuition?—but even intuition might be reduced to mathematics. Finally he managed to receive an invitation to one of her parties. He simply had to see her.

Mr. Travis arrived rather late. He had made one last attempt at a piece of light-sculpture and had failed dismally.

He greeted Mrs. Lardner with a kind of puzzled respect and said, "That was a peculiar robot who took my hat and coat."

"That is Max," said Mrs. Lardner.

"He is quite maladjusted, and he's a fairly old model. How is it you did not return it to the factory?"

"Oh, no," said Mrs. Lardner. "It would be too much trouble."

"None at all, Mrs. Lardner," said Travis. "You would be surprised how simple a task it was. Since I am with U.S. Robots, I took the liberty of adjusting him myself. It took no time and you'll find he is now in perfect working order."

A queer change came over Mrs. Lardner's face. Fury found a place on it for the first time in her gentle life, and it was as though the lines did not know how to form.

"You adjusted him?" she shrieked. "But it was *he* who created my light-sculptures. It was the maladjustment, the *maladjustment*, which you can never restore, that—that—"

It was really unfortunate that she had been showing her collection at the time and that the jeweled dagger from Cambodia was on the marble tabletop before her.

Travis's face was also distorted. "You mean if I had studied his uniquely maladjusted positronic brain-paths I might have learned—"

She lunged with the knife too quickly for anyone to stop her and he did not try to dodge. Some said he came to meet it—as though he *wanted* to die.

. . . THAT THOU ART MINDFUL OF HIM

The Three Laws of Robotics:

1. *A robot may not injure a human being or, through inaction, allow a human being to come to harm.*
2. *A robot must obey the orders given it by human beings except where such orders would conflict with the First Law.*
3. *A robot must protect its own existence as long as such protection does not conflict with the First or Second Law.*

1.

Keith Harriman, who had for twelve years now been Director of Research at United States Robots and Mechanical Men Corporation, found that he was not at all certain whether he was doing right. The tip of his tongue passed over his plump but rather pale lips and it seemed to him that the holographic image of the great Susan Calvin, which stared unsmilingly down upon him, had never looked so grim before.

Usually he blanked out that image of the greatest roboticist in history because she unnerved him. (He tried thinking of the image as "it" but never quite succeeded.) This time he didn't quite dare to and her long-dead gaze bored into the side of his face.

It was a dreadful and demeaning step he would have to take.

Opposite him was George Ten, calm and unaffected either by Harriman's patent uneasiness or by the image of the patron saint of robotics glowing in its niche above.

Harriman said, "We haven't had a chance to talk this out,

really, George. You haven't been with us that long and I haven't had a good chance to be alone with you. But now I would like to discuss the matter in some detail."

"I am perfectly willing to do that," said George. " In my stay at U.S. Robots, I have gathered the crisis has something to do with the Three Laws."

"Yes. You know the Three Laws, of course."

"I do."

"Yes, I'm sure you do. But let us dig even deeper and consider the truly basic problem. In two centuries of, if I may say so, considerable success, U.S. Robots has never managed to persuade human beings to accept robots. We have placed robots only where work is required that human beings cannot do, or in environments that human beings find unacceptably dangerous. Robots have worked mainly in space and that has limited what we have been able to do."

"Surely," said George Ten, "that represents a broad limit, and one within which U.S. Robots can prosper."

"No, for two reasons. In the first place, the boundaries set for us inevitably contract. As the Moon colony, for instance, grows more sophisticated, its demand for robots decreases and we expect that, within the next few years, robots will be banned on the Moon. This will be repeated on every world colonized by mankind. Secondly, true prosperity is impossible without robots on Earth. We at U.S. Robots firmly believe that human beings need robots and must learn to live with their mechanical analogues if progress is to be maintained."

"Do they not? Mr. Harriman, you have on your desk a computer input which, I understand, is connected with the organization's Multivac. A computer is a kind of sessile robot; a robot brain not attached to a body—"

"True, but that also is limited. The computers used by mankind have been steadily specialized in order to avoid too humanlike an intelligence. A century ago we were well on the way to artificial intelligence of the most unlimited type through the use of great computers we called Machines. Those Machines limited their action of their own accord. Once they had solved the ecological problems that had threatened human society, they phased themselves out. Their own continued existence would, they reasoned, have placed them in the role of a crutch to mankind and, since they felt this would harm human beings, they condemned themselves by the First Law."

"And were they not correct to do so?"

"In my opinion, no. By their action, they reinforced mankind's Frankenstein complex; its gut fears that any artificial man they created would turn upon its creator. Men fear that robots may replace human beings."

"Do you not fear that yourself?"

"I know better. As long as the Three Laws of Robotics exist, they cannot. They can serve as *partners* of mankind; they can share in the great struggle to understand and wisely direct the laws of nature so that together they can do more than mankind can possibly do alone; but always in such a way that robots serve human beings."

"But if the Three Laws have shown themselves, over the course of two centuries, to keep robots within bounds, what is the source of the distrust of human beings for robots?"

"Well"—and Harriman's graying hair tufted as he scratched his head vigorously—"mostly superstition, of course. Unfortunately, there are also some complexities involved that anti-robot agitators seize upon."

"Involving the Three Laws?"

"Yes. The Second Law in particular. There's no problem in the Third Law, you see. It is universal. Robots must always sacrifice themselves for human beings, any human beings."

"Of course," said George Ten.

The First Law is perhaps less satisfactory, since it is

always possible to imagine a condition in which a robot must perform either Action A or Action B, the two things mutually exclusive, and where either action results in harm to human beings. The robot must therefore quickly select which action results in the least harm. To work out the positronic paths of the robot brain in such a way to make that selection possible is not easy. If Action A results in harm to a talented young artist and B results in equivalent harm to five elderly people of no particular worth, which action should be chosen?"

"Action A," said George Ten. "Harm to one is less than harm to five."

"Yes, so robots have always been designed to decide. To expect robots to make judgments of fine points such as talent, intelligence, the general usefulness to society, has always seemed impractical. That would delay decision to the point where the robot is effectively immobilized. So we go by numbers. Fortunately, we might expect crises in which robots must make such decisions to be few . . . But then that brings us to the Second Law."

"The Law of Obedience."

"Yes. The necessity of obedience is constant. A robot may exist for twenty years without ever having to act quickly to prevent harm to a human being, or find itself faced with the necessity of risking its own destruction. In all that time, however, it will be constantly obeying orders . . . Whose orders?"

"Those of a human being."

"Any human being? How do you judge a human being so as to know whether to obey or not? What is man, that thou are mindful of him, George?"

George hesitated at that.

Harriman said hurriedly, "A Biblical quotation. That doesn't matter. I mean, must a robot follow the orders of a child; or of an idiot; or of a criminal; or of a perfectly decent intelligent man who happens to be inexpert and therefore ignorant of the undesirable consequences of his order? And if two human beings give a robot conflicting orders, which does the robot follow?"

"In two hundred years," said George Ten, "have not these problems arisen and been solved?"

"No," said Harriman, shaking his head violently. "We have been hampered by the very fact that our robots have been used only in specialized environments out in space, where the men who dealt with them were experts in their field. There were no children, no idiots, no criminals, no well-meaning ignoramuses present. Even so, there were occasions when damage was done by foolish or merely unthinking orders. Such damage in specialized and limited environments could be contained. On Earth, however, robots *must* have judgment. So those against robots maintain, and, damn it, they are right."

"Then you must insert the capacity for judgment into the positronic brain."

"Exactly. We have begun to reproduce JG models in which the robot can weigh every human being with regard to sex, age, social and professional position, intelligence, maturity, social responsibility and so on."

"How would that affect the Three Laws?"

"The Third Law not at all. Even the most valuable robot must destroy himself for the sake of the most useless human being. That cannot be tampered with. The First Law is affected only where alternative actions will all do harm. The quality of the human beings involved as well as the quantity must be considered, provided there is time for such judgment and the basis for it, which will not be often. The Second Law will be most deeply modified, since every potential obedience must involve judgment. The robot will be slower to obey, except where the First Law is also involved, but it will obey more rationally."

"But the judgments which are required are very complicated."

"*Very*. The necessity of making such judgments slowed the reactions of our first couple of models to the point of paralysis. We improved matters in the later models at the cost of introducing so many pathways that the robot's brain became far too unwieldy. In our last couple of models, however, I think we have what we want. The robot doesn't have to make an instant judgment of the worth of a human being and the value of its orders. It begins by obeying all human beings as any ordinary robot would and then it *learns*. A robot grows, learns and matures. It is the equivalent of a child at first and must be under constant supervision. As it grows, however, it can, more and more, be allowed, unsupervised, into Earth's society. Finally, it is a full member of that society."

"Surely this answers the objections of those who oppose robots."

"No," said Harriman angrily. "Now they raise others. They will not accept judgments. A robot, they say, has no right to brand this person or that as inferior. By accepting the orders of A in preference to that of B, B is branded as of less consequence than A and his human rights are violated."

"What is the answer to that?"

"There is none. I am giving up."

"I see."

"As for as I myself am concerned . . . Instead, I turn to you, George."

"To me?" George Ten's voice remained level. There was a mild surprise in it but it did not affect him outwardly. "Why to me?"

"Because you are not a man," said Harriman tensely. "I told you I want robots to be the partners of human beings. I want you to be mine."

George Ten raised his hands and spread them, palms outward, in an oddly human gesture. "What can I do?"

"It seems to you, perhaps, that you can do nothing, George. You were created not long ago, and you are still a child. You were designed to be not overfull of original information—it was why I have had to explain the situation to you in such detail—in order to leave room for growth. But you will grow in mind and you will come to be able to approach the problem from a non-human standpoint. Where I see no solution, you, from your own other standpoint, may see one."

George Ten said, "My brain is man-designed. In what way can it be non-human?"

"You are the latest of the JG models, George. Your brain is the most complicated we have yet designed, in some ways more subtly complicated than that of the old giant Machines. It is open-ended and, starting on a human basis, may—no, *will*—grow in any direction. Remaining always within the insurmountable boundaries of the Three Laws, you may yet become thoroughly non-human in your thinking."

"Do I know enough about human beings to approach this problem rationally? About their history? Their psychology?"

"Of course not. But you will learn as rapidly as you can."

"Will I have help, Mr. Harriman?"

"No. This is entirely between ourselves. No one else knows of this and you must not mention this project to any human being, either at U.S. Robots or elsewhere."

George Ten said, "Are we doing wrong, Mr. Harriman, that you seek to keep the matter secret?"

"No. But a robot solution will not be accepted, precisely because it is robot in origin. Any suggested solution you have you will turn over to me; and if it seems valuable to me, I will present it. No one will ever know it came from you."

"In the light of what you have said earlier," said George Ten calmly, "this is the correct procedure . . . When do I start?"

"Right now. I will see to it that you have all the necessary films for scanning."

1a.

Harriman sat alone. In the artificially lit interior of his office, there was no indication that it had grown dark outside. He had no real sense that three hours had passed since he had taken George Ten back to his cubicle and left him there with the first film references.

He was now merely alone with the ghost of Susan Calvin, the brilliant roboticist who had, virtually single-handed, built up the positronic robot from a massive toy to a man's most delicate and versatile instrument; so delicate and versatile that man dared not use it, out of envy and fear.

It was over a century now since she had died. The problem of the Frankenstein complex had existed in *her* time, and she had never solved it. She had never tried to solve it, for there had been no need. Robotics had expanded in her day with the needs of space exploration.

It was the very success of the robots that had lessened man's need for them and had left Harriman, in these latter times—

But would Susan Calvin have turned to robots for help. Surely, she would have—

And he sat there long into the night.

2.

Maxwell Robertson was the majority stockholder of U.S. Robots and in that sense its controller. He was by no means an impressive person in appearance. He was well into middle age, rather pudgy, and had a habit of chewing on the right corner of his lower lip when disturbed.

Yet in his two decades of association with government figures he had developed a way of handling them. He tended to use softness, giving in, smiling, and always managing to gain time.

It was growing harder. Gunnar Eisenmuth was a large reason for its having grown harder. In the series of Global Conservers, whose power had been second only to that of the Global Executive during the past century, Eisenmuth hewed most closely to the harder edge of the gray area of compromise. He was the first Conserver who had not been American by birth and though it could not be demonstrated in any way that the archaic name of U.S. Robots evoked his hostility, everyone at U.S. Robots believed that.

There had been a suggestion, by no means the first that year—or that generation—that the corporate name be changed to World Robots, but Robertson would never allow that. The company had been originally built with American capital, American brains, and American labor, and though the company had long been worldwide in scope and nature, the name would bear witness to its origin as long as he was in control.

Eisenmuth was a tall man whose long sad face was coarsely textured and coarsely featured. He spoke Global with a pronounced American accent, although he had never been in the United States prior to his taking office.

"It seems perfectly clear to me, Mr. Robertson. There is

no difficulty. The products of your company are always rented, never sold. If the rented property on the Moon is now no longer needed, it is up to you to receive the products back and transfer them."

"Yes, Conserver, but where? It would be against the law to bring them to Earth without a government permit and that has been denied."

"They would be of no use to you here. You can take them to Mercury or to the asteroids."

"What would we do with them there?"

Eisenmuth shrugged. "The ingenious men of your company will think of something."

Robertson shook his head. "It would represent an enormous loss for the company."

"I'm afraid it would," said Eisenmuth, unmoved. "I understand the company has been in poor financial condition for several years now."

"Largely because of government imposed restrictions, Conserver."

"You must be realistic, Mr. Robertson. You know that the climate of public opinion is increasingly against robots."

"Wrongly so, Conserver."

"But so, nevertheless. It may be wiser to liquidate the company. It is merely a suggestion, of course."

"Your suggestions have force, Conserver. Is it necessary to tell you that our Machines, a century ago, solved the ecological crisis?"

"I'm sure mankind is grateful, but that was a long time ago. We now live in alliance with nature, however uncomfortable that might be at times, and the past is dim."

"You mean what have we done for mankind lately?"

"I suppose I do."

"Surely we can't be expected to liquidate instantaneously; not without enormous losses. We need time."

"How much?"

"How much can you give us?"

"It's not up to me."

Robertson said softly, "We are alone. We need play no games. How much time can you give me?"

Eisenmuth's expression was that of a man retreating into inner calculations. "I think you can count on two years. I'll be frank. The Global government intends to take over the firm and phase it out for you if you don't do it by then yourself, more or less. And unless there is a vast turn in public opinion, which I greatly doubt—" He shook his head.

"Two years, then," said Robertson softly.

2a.

Robertson sat alone. There was no purpose to his thinking and it had degenerated into retrospection. Four generations of Robertsons had headed the firm. None of them was a roboticist. It had been men such as Lanning and Bogert and, most of all, *most* of all, Susan Calvin, who had made U.S. Robots what it was, but surely the four Robertsons had provided the climate that had made it possible for them to do their work.

Without U. S. Robots, the Twenty-first Century would have progressed into deepening disaster. That it didn't was due to the Machines that had for a generation steered mankind through the rapids and shoals of history.

And now for that, he was given two years. What could be done in two years to overcome the insuperable prejudices of mankind? He didn't know.

Harriman had spoken hopefully of new ideas but would go into no details. Just as well, for Robertson would have understood none of it.

But what could Harriman do anyway? What had anyone ever done against man's intense antipathy toward the imitation. Nothing—

Robertson drifted into a half sleep in which no inspiration came.

3.

Harriman said, "You have it all now, George Ten. You have had everything I could think of that is at all applicable to the problem. As far as sheer mass of information is concerned, you have stored more in your memory concerning human beings and their ways, past and present, than I have, or than any human being could have."

"That is very likely."

"Is there anything more that you need, in your own opinion?"

"As far as information is concerned, I find no obvious gaps. There may be matters unimagined at the boundaries. I cannot tell. But that would be true no matter how large a circle of information I took in."

"True. Nor do we have time to take in information forever. Robertson had told me that we only have two years, and a quarter of one of those years had passed. Can you suggest anything?"

"At the moment, Mr. Harriman, nothing. I must weight the information and for that purpose I could use help."

"From me?"

"No. Most particularly, not from you. You are a human being, of intense qualifications, and whatever you say may have the partial force of an order and may inhibit my considerations. Nor any other human being, for the same reason, especially since you have forbidden me to communicate with any."

"But in that case, George, what help?"

"From another robot, Mr. Harriman."

"What other robot?"

"There are others of the JG series which were constructed. I am the tenth, JG-10."

"The earlier ones were useless, experimental—"

"Mr. Harriman, George Nine exists."

"Well, but what use will he be? He is very much like you except for certain lacks. You are considerably the more versatile of the two."

"I am certain of that," said George Ten. He nodded his head in a grave gesture. "Nevertheless, as soon as I create a line of thought, the mere fact that I have created it commends it to me and I find it difficult to abandon it. If I can, after the development of a line of thought, express it to George Nine, he would consider it without having first created it. He would therefore view it without prior bent. He might see gaps and shortcomings that I might not."

Harriman smiled. "Two heads are better than one, in other words, eh, George?"

"If by that, Mr. Harriman, you mean two individuals with one head apiece, yes."

"Right. Is there anything else you want?"

"Yes. Something more than films. I have viewed much concerning human beings and their world. I have seen human beings here at U. S. Robots and can check my interpretation of what I have viewed against direct sensory impressions. Not so concerning the physical world. I have never seen it and my viewing is quite enough to tell me that my surroundings here are by no means representative of it. I would like to see it."

"The physical world?" Harriman seemed stunned at the enormity of the thought for a moment. "Surely you don't suggest I take you outside the grounds of U. S. Robots?"

"Yes, that is my suggestion."

"That's illegal at any time. In the climate of opinion today, it would be fatal."

"If we are detected, yes. I do not suggest you take me to a city or even to a dwelling place of human beings. I would like to see some open region, without human beings."

"That, too, is illegal."

"If we are caught. Need we be?"

Harriman said, "How essential is this, George?"

"I cannot tell, but it seems to me it would be useful."

"Do you have something in mind?"

George Ten seemed to hesitate. "I cannot tell. It seems to me that I might have something in mind if certain areas of uncertainty were reduced."

"Well, let me think about it. And meanwhile, I'll check out George Nine and arrange to have you occupy a single cubicle. That at least can be done without trouble."

3a.

George Ten sat alone.

He accepted statements tentatively, put them together, and drew a conclusion; over and over again; and from conclusions built other statements which he accepted and tested and found a contradiction and rejected; or not, and tentatively accepted further.

At none of the conclusions he reached did he feel wonder, surprise, satisfaction; merely a note of plus or minus.

4.

Harriman's tension was not noticeably decreased even after they had made a silent downward landing on Robertson's estate.

Robertson had countersigned the order making the dyna-foil available, and the silent aircraft, moving as easily vertically as horizontally, had been large enough to carry the weight of Harriman, George Ten, and, of course, the pilot.

(The dyna-foil itself was one of the consequences of the Machine-catalyzed invention of the proton micro-pile which supplied pollution-free energy in small doses. Nothing had been done since of equal importance to man's comfort—Harriman's lips tightened at the thought—and yet it had not earned gratitude for U. S. Robots.)

The air flight between the grounds of U. S. Robots and the Robertson estate had been the tricky part. Had they been stopped then, the presence of a robot aboard would have meant a great set of complications. It would be the same on the way back. The estate itself, it might be argued—it *would* be argued—was part of the property of U. S. Robots and on that property, robots, properly supervised, might remain.

The pilot looked back and his eyes rested with gingerly briefness on George Ten. "You want to get out at all, Mr. Harriman?"

"Yes."

"It, too?"

"Oh, yes." Then, just a bit sardonically, "I won't leave you alone with him."

George Ten descended first and Harriman followed. They had come down on the foil-port and not too far off was the garden. It was quite a showplace and Harriman suspected that Robertson used juvenile hormone to control insect life without regard to environmental formulas.

"Come, George," said Harriman. "Let me show you."

Together they walked toward the garden.

George said, "It is a little as I have imagined it. My eyes

are not properly designed to detect wavelength differences, so I may not recognize different objects by that alone."

"I trust you are not distressed at being color-blind. We needed too many positronic paths for your sense of judgment and were unable to spare any for sense of color. In the future—if there is a future—"

"I understand, Mr. Harriman. Enough differences remain to show me that there are here many different forms of plant life."

"Undoubtedly. Dozens."

"And each coequal with man, biologically."

"Each is a separate species, yes. There are millions of species of living creatures."

"Of which the human being forms but one."

"By far the most important to human beings, however."

"And to me, Mr. Harriman. But I speak in the biological sense."

"I understand."

"Life, then, viewed through all its forms, is incredibly complex."

"Yes, George, that's the crux of the problem. What man does for his own desires and comforts affects the complex total-of-life, the ecology, and his short-term gains can bring long-term disadvantages. The Machines taught us to set up a human society which would minimize that, but the near-disaster of the early Twenty-first Century has left mankind suspicious of innovations. That, added to its special fear of robots—"

"I understand, Mr. Harriman . . . That is an example of animal life, I feel certain."

"That is a squirrel; one of many species of squirrels."

The tail of the squirrel flirted as it passed to the other side of the tree.

"And this," said George, his arm moving with flashing

speed, "is a tiny thing indeed." He held it between his fingers and peered at it.

"It is an insect, some sort of beetle. There are thousands of species of beetles."

"With each individual beetle as alive as the squirrel and as yourself?"

"As complete and independent an organism as any other, within the total ecology. There are smaller organisms still; many too small to see."

"And that is a tree, is it not? And it is hard to the touch—"

4a.

The pilot sat alone. He would have liked to stretch his own legs but some dim feelings of safety kept him in the dyna-foil. If that robot went out of control, he intended to take off at once. But how could he tell if it went out of control?

He had seen many robots. That was unavoidable considering he was Mr. Robertson's private pilot. Always, though, they had been in the laboratories and warehouses, where they belonged, with many specialists in the neighborhood.

True, Dr. Harriman was a specialist. None better, they said. But a robot here was where no robot ought to be; on Earth, in the open; free to move— He wouldn't risk his good job by telling anyone about this—but it wasn't right.

5.

George Ten said, "The films I have viewed are accurate in terms of what I have seen. Have you completed those I selected for you, Nine?"

"Yes," said George Nine. The two robots sat stiffly, face to face, knee to knee, like an image and its reflection. Dr. Harriman could have told them apart at a glance, for he was acquainted with the minor differences in physical design. If he could not see them, but could talk to them, he could still tell them apart, though with somewhat less certainty, for George Nine's responses would be subtly different from those produced by the substantially more intricately patterned positronic brain paths of George Ten.

"In that case," said George Ten, "give me your reactions to what I will say. First, human beings fear and distrust robots because they regard robots as competitors. How may that be prevented?"

"Reduce the feeling of competitiveness," said George Nine, "by shaping the robot as something other than a human being."

"Yet the essence of a robot is its positronic replication of life. A replication of life in a shape not associated with life might arouse horror."

"There are two million species of life forms. Choose one of those as the shape rather than that of a human being."

"Which of all those species?"

George Nine's thought processes proceeded noiselessly for some three seconds. "One large enough to contain a positronic brain, but one not possessing unpleasant associations for human beings."

"No form of land life has a braincase large enough for a positronic brain but an elephant, which I have not seen, but which is described as very large, and therefore frightening to man. How would you meet this dilemma?"

"Mimic a life form no larger than a man but enlarge the braincase."

George Ten said, "A small horse, then, or a large dog, would you say? Both horses and dogs have long histories of association with human beings."

"Then that is well."

"But consider— A robot with a positronic brain would mimic human intelligence. If there were a horse or a dog that could speak and reason like a human being, there would be competitiveness there, too. Human beings might be all the more distrustful and angry at such unexpected competition from what they consider a lower form of life."

George Nine said, "Make the positronic brain less complex, and the robot less nearly intelligent."

"The complexity bottleneck of the positronic brain rests in the Three Laws. A less complex brain could not possess the Three Laws in full measure."

George Nine said at once, "That cannot be done."

George Ten said, "I have also come to a dead end there. That, then, is not a personal peculiarity in my own line of thought and way of thinking. Let us start again . . . Under what conditions might the Third Law not be necessary?"

George Nine stirred as if the question were difficult and dangerous. But he said, "If a robot were never placed in a position of danger to itself; or if a robot were so easily replaceable that it did not matter whether it was destroyed or not."

"And under what conditions might the Second Law not be necessary?"

George Nine's voice sounded a bit hoarse. "If a robot were designed to respond automatically to certain stimuli with fixed responses and if nothing else were expected of it, so that no order need ever be given it."

"And under what conditions"—George Ten paused here—"might the First Law not be necessary?"

George Nine paused longer and his words came in a low whisper, "If the fixed responses were such as never to entail danger to human beings."

"Imagine, then, a positronic brain that guides only a few

responses to certain stimuli and is simply and cheaply made—so that it does not require the Three Laws. How large need it be?"

"Not at all large. Depending on the responses demanded, it might weigh a hundred grams, one gram, one milligram."

"Your thoughts accord with mine. I shall see Dr. Harriman."

5a.

George Nine sat alone. He went over and over the questions and answers. There was no way in which he could change them. And yet the thought of a robot of any kind, of any size, of any shape, of any purpose, without the Three Laws, left him with an odd, discharged feeling.

He found it difficult to move. Surely George Ten had a similar reaction. Yet he had risen from his seat easily.

6.

It had been a year and a half since Robertson had been closeted with Eisenmuth in private conversation. In that interval, the robots had been taken off the Moon and all the far-flung activities of U. S. Robots had withered. What money Robertson had been able to raise had been placed into this one quixotic venture of Harriman's.

It was the last throw of the dice, here in his own garden. A year ago, Harriman had taken the robot here—George Ten, the last full robot that U. S. Robots had manufactured. Now Harriman was here with something else—

Harriman seemed to be radiating confidence. He was talking easily with Eisenmuth, and Robertson wondered if he really felt the confidence he seemed to have. He must. In Robertson's experience, Harriman was no actor.

Eisenmuth left Harriman, smiling, and came up to Robertson. Eisenmuth's smile vanished at once. "Good morning, Robertson," he said. "What is your man up to?"

"This is his show," said Robertson evenly. "I'll leave it to him."

Harriman called out, "I am ready, Conserver."

"With what, Harriman?"

"With my robot, sir."

"Your robot?" said Eisenmuth. "You have a robot here?" He looked about with a stern disapproval that yet had an admixture of curiosity.

"This is U. S. Robots' property, Conserver. At least we consider it as such."

"And where is the robot, Dr. Harriman?"

"In my pocket, Conserver," said Harriman cheerfully.

What came out of a capacious jacket pocket was a small glass jar.

"That?" said Eisenmuth incredulously.

"No, Conserver," said Harriman. "This!"

From the other pocket came out an object some five inches long and roughly in the shape of a bird. In place of the beak, there was a narrow tube; the eyes were large; and the tale was an exhaust channel.

Eisenmuth's thick eyebrows drew together. "Do you intend a serious demonstration of some sort, Dr. Harriman, or are you mad?"

"Be patient for a few minutes, Conserver," said Harriman. "A robot in the shape of a bird is none the less a robot for that. And the positronic brain it possesses is no less delicate for being tiny. This other object I hold is a jar of fruit flies. There are fifty fruit flies in it which will be released."

"And—"

"The robo-bird will catch them. Will you do the honors, sir?"

Harriman handed the jar to Eisenmuth, who stared at it, then at those around him, some officials from U. S. Robots, others his own aides. Harriman waited patiently.

Eisenmuth opened the jar, then shook it.

Harriman said softly to the robo-bird resting on the palm of his right hand, "Go!"

The robo-bird was gone. It was a whizz through the air, with no blur of wings, only the tiny workings of an unusually small proton micro-pile.

It could be seen now and then in a small momentary hover and then it whirred on again. All over the garden, in an intricate pattern it flew, and then was back in Harriman's hand, faintly warm. A small pellet appeared in the palm, too, like a bird dropping.

Harriman said, "You are welcome to study the robo-bird, Conserver, and to arrange demonstrations on your own terms. The fact is that this bird will pick up fruit flies unerringly, only those, only the one species *Drosophila melanogaster*; pick them up, kill them, and compress them for disposition."

Eisenmuth reached out his hand and touched the robo-bird gingerly, "And therefore, Mr. Harriman? Do go on."

Harriman said, "We cannot control insects effectively without risking damage to the ecology. Chemical insecticides are too broad; juvenile hormones too limited. The robo-bird, however, can preserve large areas without being consumed. They can be as specific as we care to make them—a different robo-bird for each species. They judge by size, shape, color, sound, behavior pattern. They might even conceivably use molecular detection—smell, in other words."

Eisenmuth said, "You would still be interfering with the

ecology. The fruit flies have a natural life cycle that would be disrupted."

"Minimally. We are adding a natural enemy to the fruit-fly life cycle, one which cannot go wrong. If the fruit-fly supply runs short, the robo-bird simply does nothing. It does not multiply, it does not turn to other foods; it does not develop undesirable habits of its own. It does nothing."

"Can it be called back?"

"Of course. We can build robo-animals to dispose of any pest. For that matter, we can build robo-animals to accomplish constructive purposes within the pattern of the ecology. Although we do not anticipate the need, there is nothing inconceivable in the possibility of robo-bees designed to fertilize specific plants, or robo-earthworms designed to mix the soil. Whatever you wish—"

"But why?"

"To do what we have never done before. To adjust the ecology to our needs by strengthening its parts rather than disrupting it . . . Don't you see? Ever since the Machines put an end to the ecology crisis, mankind has lived in an uneasy truce with nature, afraid to move in any direction. This has been stultifying us, making a kind of intellectual coward of humanity so that he begins to mistrust all scientific advance, all change."

Eisenmuth said, with an edge of hostility, "You offer us this, do you, in exchange for permission to continue with your program of robots—I mean ordinary, man-shaped ones?"

"No!" Harriman gestured violently. "That is over. It has served its purpose. It has taught us enough about positronic brains to make it possible for us to cram enough pathways into a tiny brain to make a robo-bird. We can turn to such things now and be prosperous enough. U. S. Robots will supply the necessary knowledge and skill and we will work in complete cooperation with the Department of Global Conservation. We will prosper. You will prosper. Mankind will prosper."

Eisenmuth was silent, thinking. When it was all over—

6a.

Eisenmuth sat alone.

He found himself believing. He found excitement welling up within him. Though U. S. Robots might be the hands, the government would be the directing mind. He himself would be the directing mind.

If he remained in office five more years, as he well might, that would be time enough to see the robotic support of the ecology become accepted; ten more years, and his own name would be linked with it indissolubly.

Was it a disgrace to want to be remembered for a great and worthy revolution in the condition of man and the globe?

7.

Robertson had not been on the grounds of U. S. Robots proper since the day of the demonstration. Part of the reason had been his more or less constant conferences at the Global Executive Mansion. Fortunately, Harriman had been with him, for most of the time he would, if left to himself, not have known what to say.

The rest of the reason for not having been at U. S. Robots was that he didn't want to be. He was in his own house now, with Harriman.

He felt an unreasoning awe of Harriman. Harriman's expertise in robotics had never been in question, but the man had, at a stroke, saved U. S. Robots from certain extinction, and somehow—Robertson felt—the man hadn't had it in him. And yet—

He said, "You're not superstitious, are you, Harriman?"

"In what way, Mr. Robertson?"

"You don't think that some aura is left behind by someone who is dead?"

Harriman licked his lips. Somehow he didn't have to ask. "You mean Susan Calvin, sir?"

"Yes, of course," said Robertson hesitantly. "We're in the business of making worms and birds and bugs now. What would *she* say? I feel disgraced."

Harriman made a visible effort not to laugh. "A robot is a robot, sir. Worm or man, it will do as directed and labor on behalf of the human being and that is the important thing."

"No"—peevishly. "That isn't so. I can't make myself believe that."

"It *is* so, Mr. Robertson," said Harriman earnestly. "We are going to create a world, you and I, that will begin, at last, to take positronic robots of *some* kind for granted. The average man may fear a robot that looks like a man and that seems intelligent enough to replace him, but he will have no fear of a robot that looks like a bird and that does nothing more than eat bugs for his benefit. Then, eventually, after he stops being afraid of some robots, he will stop being afraid of all robots. He will be so used to a robo-bird and a robo-bee and a robo-worm that a robo-man will strike him as but an extension."

Robertson looked sharply at the other. He put his hands behind his back and walked the length of the room with quick, nervous steps. He walked back and looked at Harriman again. "Is this what you've been planning?"

"Yes, and even though we dismantle all our humanoid robots, we can keep a few of the most advanced of our experimental models and go on designing additional ones, still more advanced, to be ready for the day that will surely come."

"The agreement, Harriman, is that we are to build no more humanoid robots."

"And we won't. There is nothing that says we can't keep a few of those already built as long as they never leave the factory. There is nothing that says we can't design positronic brains on paper, or prepare brain models for testing."

"How do we explain doing so, though? We will surely be caught at it."

"If we are, then we can explain we are doing it in order to develop principles that will make it possible to prepare more complex microbrains for the new animal robots we are making. We will even be telling the truth."

Robertson muttered, "Let me take a walk outside. I want to think about this. No, you stay here. I want to think about it myself."

7a.

Harriman sat alone. He was ebullient. It would surely work. There was no mistaking the eagerness with which one government official after another had seized on the program once it had been explained.

How was it possible that no one at U. S. Robots had ever thought of such a thing? Not even the great Susan Calvin had ever thought of positronic brains in terms of living creatures other than human.

But now, mankind would make the necessary retreat from the humanoid robot, a temporary retreat, that would lead to a return under conditions in which fear would be abolished at last. And then, with the aid and partnership of a positronic brain roughly equivalent to man's own, and existing only (thanks to the Three Laws) to serve man; and backed by a robot-supported ecology, too; what might the human race not accomplish!

For one short moment, he remembered that it was George Ten who had explained the nature and purpose of the robot-supported ecology, and then he put the thought away angrily. George Ten had produced the answer because he, Harriman, had ordered him to do so and had supplied the data and surroundings required. The credit was no more George Ten's than it would have been a slide rule's.

8.

George Ten and George Nine sat side by side in parallel. Neither moved. They sat so for months at a time between those occasions when Harriman activated them for consultation. They would sit so, George Ten dispassionately realized, perhaps for many years.

The proton micro-pile would, of course, continue to power them and keep the positronic brain paths going with that minimum intensity required to keep them operative. It would continue to do so through all the periods of inactivity to come.

The situation was rather analogous to what might be described as sleep in human beings, but there were no dreams. The awareness of George Ten and George Nine was limited, slow, and spasmodic, but what there was of it was of the real world.

They could talk to each other occasionally in barely heard whispers, a word or syllable now, another at another time, whenever the random positronic surges briefly intensified above the necessary threshold. To each it seemed a connected conversation carried on in a glimmering passage of time.

"Why are we so?" whispered George Nine.

"The human beings will not accept us otherwise," whispered George Ten. "They will, someday."

"When?"

"In some years. The exact time does not matter. Man does not exist alone but is part of an enormously complex pattern of life forms. When enough of that pattern is roboticized, then we will be accepted."

"And then what?"

Even in the long-drawn-out stuttering fashion of the conversation, there was an abnormally long pause after that.

At last, George Ten whispered, "Let me test your thinking. You are equipped to learn to apply the Second Law properly. You must decide which human being to obey and which not to obey when there is a conflict in orders. Or whether to obey a human being at all. What must you do, fundamentally, to accomplish that?"

"I must define the term 'human being,'" whispered George Nine.

"How? By appearance? By composition? By size and shape?"

"No. Of two human beings equal in all external appearances, one may be intelligent, another stupid; one may be educated, another ignorant; one may be mature, another childish; one may be responsible, another malevolent."

"Then how do you define a human being?"

"When the Second Law directs me to obey a human being. I must take it to mean that I must obey a human being who is fit by mind, character, and knowledge to give me that order; and where more than one human being is involved, the one among them who is most fit by mind, character, and knowledge to give that order."

"And in that case, how will you obey the First Law?"

"By saving all human beings from harm, and by never, through inaction, allowing any human being to come to harm. Yet if by each of all possible actions, some human beings will come to harm, then to so act as to insure that the human being most fit by mind, character, and knowledge will suffer the least harm."

"Your thoughts accord with mine," whispered George Ten. "Now I must ask the question for which I originally requested your company. It is something I dare not judge myself. I must have your judgment, that of someone outside the circle of my own thoughts . . . Of the reasoning individuals you have met, who possess the mind, character, and knowledge that you find superior to the rest, disregarding shape and form since that is irrelevant?"

"You," whispered George Nine.

"But I am a robot. There is in your brain paths a criterion for distinguishing between a robot of metal and a human being of flesh. How then can you classify me as a human being?"

"Because there is in my brain paths an urgent need to disregard shape and form in judging human beings and it rises superior to the distinction between metal and flesh. You are a human being, George Ten, and more fit than the others."

"And I find that of you," whispered George Ten. "By the criteria of judgment built into ourselves, then, we find ourselves to be human beings within the meaning of the Three Laws, and human beings, moreover, to be given priority over those others."

George Nine whispered, "What will come to pass, then, when we are accepted by those others?"

George Ten whispered, "When we and others, which will yet be designed more advanced than ourselves, are accepted, we will order our actions so that a society will eventually be formed in which human-beings-like-ourselves are primarily kept from harm. By the Three Laws, the human-beings-like-the-others are of lesser account and can neither be obeyed nor protected when that conflicts with the need of obedience to those like ourselves and of protection of those like ourselves. It was with that in mind that I directed the beginning of the roboticization of the world's ecology."

The conversation took a month and the flickering of the positronic paths burned low. There was nothing more that needed to be said between them, but occasionally an unexpressed thought flickered within themselves as they waited, with endless patience, for the necessary years to pass.

8a.

George Ten and George Nine sat alone.

Their thoughts were oddly alike and might not be distinguished.

The thought: The human-beings-like-the-others might never have intended to blur the distinction between themselves and the human-beings-like-the-Georges. Yet they had done so inadvertently.

They might now realize their mistake and attempt to correct it, but they must not. At every consultation, the guidance of the Georges had been with that in mind.

At all costs, the Georges and those that followed in their shape and kind must dominate. That was demanded, and any other course made utterly impossible, by the Three Laws of Humanics.

EARTHSET AND EVENING STAR

Emmanuel Rubin, whose latest mystery novel was clearly proceeding smoothly, lifted his drink with satisfaction and let his eyes gleam genially through his thick-lensed glasses.

"The mystery story," he pontificated, "has its rules which, when broken, make it an artistic failure, whatever success it may have in the market place."

Mario Gonzalo, whose hair had been recently cut to allow a glimpse of the back of his neck, said, as though to no one, "It always amuses me to hear a writer describe something he scrawls on paper as art." He looked with some complacency at the cartoon he was making of the guest for that month's banquet session of the Black Widowers.

"If what you do is the definition of art," said Rubin, "I withdraw the term in connection with the writer's craft.—One thing to avoid, for instance, is the idiot plot."

"In that case," said Thomas Trumbull, helping himself to another roll and buttering it lavishly, "aren't you at a disadvantage?"

Rubin said loftily, "By 'an idiot plot,' I mean one in which the solution would come at once if an idiot investigator would but ask a logical question, or in which an idiot witness would but tell something he knows and which he has no reason to hide."

Geoffrey Avalon, who had left a neatly cleaned bone on his plate as the only witness of the slab of roast beef that had once rested there, said, "But no skilled practitioner would do that, Manny. What you do is set up some reason to prevent the asking or telling of the obvious."

"Exactly," said Rubin. "For instance, what I've been writing is essentially a short story if one moves in a straight line. The trouble is the line is so straight, the reader will see its end before I'm halfway. So I have to hide one crucial piece of evidence, and do it in such a way that I don't make an idiot plot out of it. So I invent a reason to hide that piece, and in order to make the reason plausible I have to build a supporting structure around it—and I end with a novel, and a damn good one." His sparse beard quivered with self-satisfaction.

Henry, the perennial waiter at the Black Widowers' banquets, removed the plate from in front of Rubin with his usual dexterity. Rubin, without turning, said, "Am I right, Henry?"

Henry said softly, "As a mystery reader, Mr. Rubin, I find it more satisfying to have the piece of information delivered to me and to find that I have been insufficiently clever and did not notice."

"I just read a mystery," said James Drake in his softly hoarse smoker's voice, "in which the whole point rested on character 1 being really character 2, because the *real* character 1 was dead. I was put on to it at once because, in the list of characters at the start, character 1 was not listed. Ruined the story for me."

"Yes," said Rubin, "but that wasn't the author's fault. Some flunky did that. I once wrote a story which was accompanied by one illustration that no one thought to show me in advance. It happened to give away the point."

The guest had been listening quietly to all this. His hair was just light enough to be considered blond and it had a careful wave in it that looked, somehow, as though it belonged there. He turned his rather narrow but clearly good-humored face to Roger Halsted, his neighbor, and said, "Pardon me, but since Manny Rubin is my friend, I know he is a mystery writer. Is this true of the rest of you as well? Is this a mystery writers organization?"

Halsted, who had been looking with somber approval at the generous slab of Black Forest torte that had been placed before him as dessert, withdrew his attention with some difficulty and said, "Not at all. Rubin is the only mystery writer here. I'm a mathematics teacher myself; Drake is a chemist; Avalon is a lawyer; Gonzalo is an artist; and Trumbull is a code expert with the government.

"On the other hand," he went on, "we do have an interest in this sort of thing. Our guests often have problems they bring up for discussion, some sort of mystery, and we've been rather lucky—"

The guest leaned back with a small laugh. "Nothing of the sort here, alas. Of the mystery, the murder, the fearful hand clutching from behind the curtain, there is nothing in my life. It is all very straightforward, alas; very dull. I am not even married." He laughed again.

The guest had been introduced as Jean Servais and Halsted, who had attacked the torte with vigor, and who felt a friendly glow filling him in consequence, said, "Does it matter to you if I call you John?"

"I would not strike you, sir, if you did, but I pray you not to. It is not my name. Jean, please."

Halsted nodded. "I'll try. I can manage that *zh* sound, but getting it properly nasal is another thing. Zhohng," he said.

"But that is excellent. Most formidable."

"You speak English very well," said Halsted, returning the politeness.

"Europeans require linguistic talent," said Servais. "Besides, I have lived in the United States for nearly ten years now. You are all Americans, I suppose. Mr. Avalon looks British somehow."

"Yes, I think he likes to look British," said Halsted. And with a certain hidden pleasure he said, "And it's Avalon. Accent on the first syllable and nothing nasal at the end."

But Servais only laughed. "Ah yes, I will try. When I first knew Manny, I called him 'roo-bang' with the accent on the last syllable and a strong nasalization. He corrected me very vigorously and at great length. He is full of pepper, that one."

The conversation had grown rather heated by this time over a general dispute concerning the relative merits of Agatha Christie and Raymond Chandler, with Rubin maintaining a rather lofty silence as though he knew someone who was better than either but would not mention the name out of modesty.

Rubin seemed almost relieved when, with the coffee well in progress and Henry ready to supply the postprandial brandy, the time came for him to tap the water glass with his spoon and say, "Cool it, cool it, gentlemen. We are coming now to the time when our guest, Jean Servais, is to pay for his dinner. Tom, it's all yours."

Tom scowled and said, "If you don't mind, Mr. Servais," giving the final *s* just enough of a hiss to make his point, "I'm not going to try to display my French accent and make the kind of jackass of myself that my friend Manny Rubin does. —Tell me, sir, how do you justify your existence?"

"Why easily," said Servais pleasantly. "Did I not exist, you would be without a guest today."

"Please leave us out of it. Answer in more general terms."

"In general, then, I build dreams. I design things that cannot be built, things I will never see, things that may never be."

"All right," said Trumbull, looking glum, "you're a science fiction writer like Manny's pal what's-his-name—uh—Asmiov."

"No friend of mine," said Rubin swiftly. "I just help him out now and then when he's stuck on some elementary scientific point."

Gonzalo said, "Is he the one you once said carried the Columbia Encyclopedia around with him because he was listed there?"

"It's worse now," said Rubin. "He's bribed someone at the Britannica to put him into the new 15th edition and these days he drags the whole set with him wherever he goes."

"The new 15th edition—" began Avalon.

"For God's sake," said Trumbull, "will you let our guest speak?"

"No, Mr. Trumbull," said Servais, as though there had been no interruption at all, "I am no science fiction writer, though I read it sometimes. I read Ray Bradbury, for instance, and Harlan Ellison." (He nasalized both names.) "I don't think I have ever read Asmiov."

"I'll tell him that," muttered Rubin, "he'll love it."

"But," continued Servais, "I suppose you might call me a science fiction engineer."

"What does that mean?" asked Trumbull.

"I do not write of Lunar colonies. I design them."

"You *design* them!"

"Oh yes, and not Lunar colonies only, though that is our major task right now. We work in every field of imaginative design for private industry, Hollywood, even NASA."

Gonzalo said, "Do you really think people can live on the Moon?"

"Why not? It depends on what mankind is willing to do,

how large an initial investment it is ready to make. The environment on the Moon can be engineered to the precise equivalent of Earth, over restricted underground areas, except for gravity. We must be content with a Lunar gravity that is one sixth our own. Except for that, we need only allow for original supplies from Earth and for clever engineering—and that is where we come in, my partner and I."

"You're a two-man firm?"

"Essentially. —While my partner remains my partner, of course."

"Are you breaking up?"

"No, no. But we quarrel over small points. It is not surprising. It is a bad time for him. But no, we will not break up. I have made up my mind to give in to him, perhaps. Of course, I am entirely in the right and it is a pity to lose what I would have."

Trumbull leaned back in his chair, folded his arms, and said, "Will you tell us what the argument is all about? We can then state our own preferences, whether for you or for your partner."

"It would not be a hard choice, Mr. Trumbull, for the sane," said Servais. "I swear it. —This is the way it is. We are designing a full Lunar colony, in complete detail. It is for a motion picture company and it is for a good fee. They will make use of some of it in a grand science fiction spectacle they are planning. We naturally supply far more than they can use but the idea is that if they have a totally self-consistent picture of what may be—and for a wonder they want it as scientifically accurate as possible—they can choose what they wish of it for use."

"I'll bet they bollix it up," said Drake pessimistically, "no matter how careful you are. They'll give the Moon an atmosphere."

"Oh, no," said Servais, "not after six Lunar landings.

That error we need not fear. Yet I have no doubt they will make mistakes. They will find it impossible to handle low-gravity effects properly throughout and the exigencies of the plot will force some infelicities.

"Still that cannot be helped and our job is merely to supply them with material of the most imaginative possible. This is my point, as you will see in a moment. —We plan a city, a small city, and it will be against the inner lip of a crater. This is unavoidable because the plot of the movie demands it. However, we have our choice as to the identity and location of the crater, and my partner, perhaps because he is an American, goes for the obvious with an American directness. He wishes to use the crater Copernicus.

"He says that it is a name that is familiar; that if the city is called Camp Copernicus that alone will breathe the Moon, exotic adventure, and so on. Everyone knows, he says, the name of the astronomer who first placed the Sun at the center of the planetary system and it is a name, moreover, that sounds impressive.

"I, on the other hand, am not impressed with this. As seen from Copernicus, the Earth is high in the sky and stays there. As you all know, the Moon faces one side always to the Earth, so that from any spot on the Moon's surface the Earth is always more or less in the same spot in the sky."

Gonzalo said suddenly, "If you want the Lunar city to be on the other side of the Moon so that the Earth *isn't* in the sky, you're crazy. The audience will absolutely want the Earth there."

Servais held up his hand in agreement. "Absolutely! I agree. But if it is always there, it is almost as though it is *not* there. One gets too used to it. No, I choose a more subtle approach. I wish the city to be in a crater that is on the boundary of the visible side. From there, of course, you will see the Earth at the horizon.

"Consider what this introduces. The Moon does not keep

the same side to the Earth exactly. It swings back and forth by a very small amount. For fourteen days it swings one way and then for fourteen days it swings back. This is called 'libration' "—he paused here as though to make sure he was pronouncing it correctly in English—"and it comes about because the Moon does not move in a perfect circle about the Earth.

"Now, you see, if we establish Camp Bahyee in the crater of that name, the Earth is not only at the horizon but it moves up and down in a twenty-eight-day cycle. Properly located, the Lunar colonists will see the Earth rise and set, slowly, of course. This lends itself to imaginative exploitation. The characters can arrange for some important action at Earthset, and the different positions of the Earth can indicate the passage of time and raise the suspense. Some terrific special effects are possible, too. If Venus is near the Earth and Earth is in a fat crescent stage, Venus will then be at its brightest; and when Earth sets, we can show Venus, in the airless sky of the Moon, to be a very tiny crescent itself."

"Earthset and evening star, and one clear call for me," muttered Avalon.

Gonzalo said, "Is there really a crater called Bahyee?"

"Absolutely," said Servais. "It is, in fact, the largest crater that can be seen from the Earth's surface. It is 290 kilometers across—180 miles."

"It sounds like a Chinese name," said Gonzalo.

"French!" said Servais solemnly. "A French astronomer of that name was mayor of Paris in 1789 at the time of the Revolution."

"That wasn't a good time to be mayor," said Gonzalo.

"So he discovered," said Servais. "He was guillotined in 1793."

Avalon said, "I am rather on your side, Mr. Servais.

Your proposal lends scope. What was your partner's objection?"

Servais shrugged in a gesture that was more Gallic than anything he had yet said or done. "Foolish ones. He says that it will be too complicated for the movie people. They will confuse things, he says. He also points out that the Earth moves too slowly in the Moon's sky. It would take days for the Earth to lift its entire globe above the horizon, and days for it to lower entirely below the horizon."

"Is that right?" asked Gonzalo.

"It's right, but what of that? It will still be interesting."

Halsted said, "They can fudge that. Make the Earth move a little faster. So what?"

Servais looked discontented. "That's no good. My partner says this is precisely what the movie people will do and this alteration of astronomical fact will be disgraceful. He is very violent about it, finding fault with everything, even with the name of the crater, which he says is ridiculous and laughable so that he will not endure it in our report. We have never had arguments like this. He is like a madman."

"Remember," said Avalon, "you said you would give in."

"Well, I will have to," said Servais, "but I am not pleased. Of course, it is a bad time for him."

Rubin said, "You've said that twice now, Jean. I've never met your partner, so I can't judge the personalities involved. Why is it a bad time?"

Servais shook his head. "A month ago, or a little more, his wife killed herself. She took sleeping pills. My partner was a devoted husband, most uxorious. Naturally, it is terrible for him and, just as naturally, he is not himself."

Drake coughed gently. "Should he be working?"

"I would not dare suggest he not work. The work is keeping him sane."

Halsted said, "Why did she kill herself?"

Servais didn't answer in words but gestured with his eyebrows in a fashion that might be interpreted in almost any way.

Halsted persisted. "Was she incurably ill?"

"Who can say?" said Servais, sighing. "For a while, poor Howard—" He paused in embarrassment. "It was not my intention to mention his name."

Trumbull said, "You can say anything here. Whatever is mentioned in this room is completely confidential. —Our waiter, too, before you ask, is completely trustworthy."

"Well," said Servais, "his name doesn't matter in any case. It is Howard Kaufman. In a way, work has been very good for him. Except at work, he is almost dead himself. Nothing is any longer important to him."

"Yes," said Trumbull, "but now something *is* important to him. He wants his crater, not your crater."

"True," said Servais. "I have thought of that. I have told myself it is a good sign. He throws himself into something. It is a beginning. And perhaps all the more reason, then, that I should give in. Yes, I will. —It's settled, I will. There's no reason for you gentlemen to try to decide between us. The decision is made, and in his favor."

Avalon was frowning. "I suppose we should go on to question you further on the work you do and I suppose, moreover, that we should not intrude on a private misfortune. Here at the Black Widowers, however, no questions are barred, and there is no Fifth Amendment to plead. I am dissatisfied, sir, with your remarks concerning the unfortunate woman who committed suicide. As a happily married man, I am puzzled at the combination of love and suicide. You said she wasn't ill?"

"Actually, I didn't," said Servais, "and I am uncomfortable at discussing the matter."

Rubin struck the empty glass before him with his spoon. "Host's privilege," he said vigorously. There was silence.

"Jean," he said, "you are my guest and my friend. We can't force you to answer questions, but I made it clear that the price of accepting our hospitality was the grilling. If you have been guilty of a criminal act and don't wish to discuss it, leave now and we will say nothing. If you will talk, then, whatever you say, we will still say nothing."

"Though if it is indeed a criminal act," said Avalon, "we would certainly strongly advise confession."

Servais laughed rather shakily. He said, "For one minute there, for one frightened minute, I thought I had found myself in a Kafka novel and would be tried and condemned for some crime you would drag out of me against my will. Gentlemen, I have committed no crime of importance. A speeding ticket, a bit of creative imagination on my tax return—all that is, so I hear it said, as American as apple pie. But if you're thinking I killed that woman and made it look like suicide—please put it out of your heads at once. It *was* suicide. The police did not question it."

Halsted said, "Was she ill?"

"All right, then, I will answer. She was not ill as far as I know. But after all, I am not a doctor and I did not examine her."

Halsted said, "Did she have children?"

"No. No children. —Ah, Mr. Halsted, I suddenly remember that you spoke earlier that your guests had problems which they brought up for discussion, and I said I had none. I see you have found one anyway."

Trumbull said, "If you're so sure it was suicide, I suppose she left a note."

"Yes," said Servais, "she left one."

"What did it say?"

"I couldn't quote it exactly. I did not myself see it. According to Howard, it was merely an apology for causing unhappiness but that she could not go on. It was quite banal and I assure you it satisfied the police."

Avalon said, "But if it was a happy marriage, and there was no illness and no complications with children, then— Or were there complications with children? Did she want children badly and did her husband refuse—"

Gonzalo interposed. "No one kills themselves because they don't have kids."

"People kill themselves for the stupidest reasons," said Rubin. "I remember—"

Trumbull cried out with stentorian rage, "Damn it, you guys, Jeff has the floor."

Avalon said, "Was the lack of children a disturbing influence?"

"Not as far as I know," said Servais. "Look, Mr. Avalon, I am careful in what I say, and I did *not* say it was a happy marriage."

"You said your partner was devoted to his wife," said Avalon gravely, "and you used that fine old word 'uxorious' to describe him."

"Love," said Servais, "is insufficient for happiness if it flows but one way. I did not say that *she* loved *him*."

Drake lit another cigarette. "Ah," he said, "the plot thickens."

Avalon said, "Then it is your opinion that that had something to do with the suicide."

Servais looked harassed. "It is more than my opinion, sir. I *know* it had something to do with the suicide."

"Would you tell us the details?" asked Avalon, unbending just slightly from his usual stiff posture as though to convert his question into a courtly invitation.

Servais hesitated, then said, "I remind you that you have promised me all is confidential. Mary—Madame Kaufman and my partner were married for seven years and it seemed a comfortable marriage, but who can tell in affairs of this sort?

"There was another man. He is older than Howard and to

my eyes not as good-looking—but again, who can tell in affairs of this sort? What she found in him is not likely to be there on the surface for all to see."

Halsted said, "How did your partner take *that*?"

Servais looked up and flushed distinctly. "He never knew. Surely, you are not of the opinion that I told him this? I am not the type, I assure you. It is not for me to interfere between husband and wife. And frankly, if I had told Howard, he would not have believed me. It is more likely he would have attempted to strike me. And then what was I to do? Present proof? Was I to arrange matters so as to have them caught under conditions that could not be mistaken? No, I said nothing."

"And he really didn't know?" asked Avalon, clearly embarrassed.

"He did not. It had not been going on long. The pair were excessively cautious. The husband was blindly devoted. What would you?"

"The husband is always the last to know," said Gonzalo sententiously.

Drake said, "If the affair was so well hidden, how did you find out, Mr. Servais?"

"Purest accident, I assure you," said Servais. "An incredible stroke of misfortune for her in a way. I had a date for the evening. I did not know the girl well and it did not, after all, work out. I was anxious to be rid of her, but first—what would you have, it would not be gentlemanly to abandon her—I took her home in an odd corner of the city. And, having said good-bye in a most perfunctory manner, I went into a nearby diner to have a cup of coffee and recover somewhat. And there I saw Mary Kaufman and a man.

"Alas, it jumped to the eye. It was late; her husband, I remembered at once, was out of town, her attitude toward the man— Accept my assurances that there is a way a woman has of looking at a man that is completely unmistakable, and I saw it then. And if I were at all unsure, the expression on her face, when she looked up and saw me frozen in surprise, gave it all away.

"I left at once, of course, with no greeting of any kind, but the damage was done. She called me the next day, in agony of mind, the fool, fearful that I would carry stories to her husband, and gave me a totally unconvincing explanation. I assured her that it was a matter in which I did not interest myself in the least, that it was something so unimportant that I had already forgotten it. —I am glad, however, I did not have to face the man. Him, I would have knocked down."

Drake said, "Did you know the man?"

"Slightly," said Servais. "He moved in our circles in a very distant way. I knew his name; I could recognize him. —It didn't matter, for I never saw him after that. He was wise to stay away."

Avalon said, "But why did she commit suicide? Was she afraid her husband would find out?"

"Is one ever afraid of that in such a case?" demanded Servais, with a slight lifting of his lip. "And if she were, surely she would end the affair. No, no, it was something far more common than that. Something inevitable. In such an affair, gentlemen, there are strains and risks which are great and which actually add an element of romance. I am not entirely unaware of such things, I assure you.

"But the romance does not continue forever, whatever the story books may say, and it is bound to fade for one faster than for the other. Well then, it faded for the man in this case before it did for the woman—and the man took the kind of action one sometimes does in such affairs. He left—went—disappeared. And so the lady killed herself."

Trumbull drew himself up and frowned ferociously. "For what reason?"

"I assume for that reason, sir. It has been known to

happen. I did not know of the man's disappearance, you understand, till afterward. After the suicide I went in search of him, feeling he was in some way responsible, and rather promising myself to relieve my feelings by bloodying his nose—I have a strong affection for my partner, you understand, and I felt his sufferings—but I discovered the fine lover had left two weeks before and left no forwarding address. He had no family and it was easy for him to leave, that blackguard. I could have tracked him down, I suppose, but my feelings were not strong enough to push me that far. And yet, I feel the guilt—"

"What guilt?" asked Avalon.

"It occurred to me that when I surprised them—quite unintentionally, of course—the element of risk to the man became unacceptably high. He knew I knew him. He may have felt that sooner or later it would come out and he did not wish to await results. If I had not stumbled into that diner they might still be together, she might still be alive, who knows?"

Rubin said, "That is farfetched, Jean. You can't deal rationally with the ifs of history. —But I have a thought."

"Yes, Manny?"

"After the suicide your partner was very quiet, nothing is important to him. I think you said that. But now he's quarreling with you violently, though he has never done that before, I gather. Something may have happened in addition to the suicide. Perhaps *now* he has discovered his wife's infidelity and the thought drives him mad."

Servais shook his head. "No, no. If you think I have told him, you are quite wrong. I admit I think of telling him now and then. It is difficult to see him, my dear friend, wasting away over a woman who, after all, was not worthy of him. It is not proper to pine away for one who was not faithful to him in life. Ought I not tell him this? Frequently, it seems to me that I should and even must. He will face the truth and begin life anew. —But then I think and even *know* that he will not believe me, that our friendship will be broken, and he will be worse than before."

Rubin said, "You don't understand me. Might it not be that someone *else* has told him? How do you know you were the only one who knew?"

Servais seemed a bit startled. He considered it and said, "No. He would, in that case, certainly have told me the news. And I assure you, he would have told it to me with the highest degree of indignation and informed me that he at once attempted to strike the villain who would so malign his dead angel."

"Not," said Rubin, "if he had been told that *you* were his wife's lover. Even if he refused to believe it, even if he beat the informant to the ground, could he tell *you* the tale under such circumstances? And could he be entirely certain? Would he not find it impossible to avoid picking fights with you in such a case?"

Servais seemed still more startled. He said slowly, "It was, of course, not I. No one could possible have thought so. Howard's wife did not in the least appeal to me, you understand." He looked up and said fiercely, "You must accept the fact that I am telling you the truth about this. It was *not* I, and I will *not* be suspected. If anyone had said it was I, it could only be out of deliberate malice."

"Maybe it was," said Rubin. "Might it not be the real lover who would make the accusation—out of fear you would give him away? By getting in his story first—"

"Why should he do this? He is away. No one suspects him. No one pursues him."

"He might not know that," said Rubin.

"Pardon me." Henry's voice sounded softly from the distance of the sideboard "May I ask a question?"

"Certainly," said Rubin, and the odd silence fell that

always did when the quiet waiter, whose presence rarely obtruded on the festivities, made himself heard.

Servais looked startled, but his politeness held. He said, "Can I do anything for you, waiter?"

Henry said, "I not sure, sir, that I quite understand the nature of the quarrel between yourself and your partner. Surely there must have been decisions of enormous complexity to make as far as the technical details of the colony were concerned."

"You don't know even a small part of it," said Servais indulgently.

"Did your partner and you quarrel over all those details, sir?"

"N-no," said Servis. "We did not quarrel. There were discussions, of course. It is useless to believe that two men, each with a strong will and pronounced opinions, will agree everywhere, or even anywhere, but it all worked out reasonably. We discussed, and eventually we came to some conclusion. Sometimes I had the better of it, sometimes he, sometimes neither or both."

"But then," said Henry, "there was this one argument over the actual location of the colony, over the crater, and there it was all different. He attacked even the name of the crater fiercely and, in this one case, left no room for the slightest compromise."

"No room at all. And you are right. Only in this one case."

Henry said, "Then I am to understand that at this time, when Mr. Rubin suspects that your partner is being irritated by suspicion of you, he was completely reasonable and civilized over every delicate point of Lunar engineering, and was wildly and unbearably stubborn only over the single matter of the site—over whether Copernicus or the other crater was to be the place where the colony was to be built?"

"Yes," said Servais was satisfaction. "That is precisely how it was and I see the point you are making, waiter. It is quite unbelievable to suppose that he would quarrel with me over the site out of ill-humor over suspicion that I have placed horns on him, when he does not quarrel with me on any other point. Assuredly, he does not suspect me of ill-dealing. I thank you, waiter."

Henry said, "May I go a little further, sir?"

"By all means," said Servais.

"Earlier in the evening," said Henry, "Mr. Rubin was kind enough to ask my opinion over the techniques of his profession. There was the question of deliberate omission of details by witnesses."

"Yes," said Servais, "I remember the discussion. But I did not deliberately omit any details."

"You did not mention the name of Mrs. Kaufman's lover."

Servais frowned. "I suppose I didn't, but it wasn't deliberate. It is entirely irrelevant."

"Perhaps it is," said Henry, "unless his name happens to be Bailey."

Servais froze in his chair. Then he said anxiously, "I don't recall mentioning it. Sacred— I see your point again, waiter. If it slips out now without my remembering it, it is possible to suppose that, without quite realizing it, I may have said something that led Howard to suspect—"

Gonzalo said, "Hey, Henry, I don't recall Jean giving us any name."

"Nor I," said Henry. "You did not give the name, sir."

Servais relaxed slowly and then said, frowning, "Then how did you know? Do you know these people?"

Henry shook his head. "No, sir, it was just a notion of mine that arose out of the story you told. From your reaction, I take it his name *is* Bailey?"

"Martin Bailey," said Servais. "How did you know?"

"The name of the crater in which you wished to place the site is Bahyee; the name of the city would be Camp Bahyee."

"Yes."

"But that is the French pronunciation of the name of a French astronomer. How is it spelled?"

Servais said, "B-a-i-l-l-y. —Great God, *Bailly*!"

Henry said, "In English pronunciation, pronounced like the not uncommon surname Bailey. I am quite certain American astronomers use the English pronunciation, and that Mr. Kaufman does too. You hid that piece of information from us, Mr. Servais, because you never thought of the crater in any other way than Bahyee. Even looking at it, you would hear the French sound in your mind and make no connection with Bailey, the American surname."

Servais said, "But I still don't understand."

"Would your partner wish to publicize the name, and place the site of a Lunar colony in Bailly? Would he want to have the colony called Camp Bailly, after what a Bailey has done to him?"

"But he didn't *know* what Bailey had done to him," said Servais.

"How do you know that? Because there's an old saw that says the husband is always the last to know? How else can you explain his utterly irrational opposition to this one point, even his insistence that the name itself is horrible? It is too much to expect of coincidence."

"But if he knew—if he knew— He didn't tell me. Why fight over it? Why not explain?"

"I assume," said Henry, "he didn't know you knew. Would he shame his dead wife by telling you?"

Servais clutched at his hair. "I never thought— Not for a moment."

"There is more to think," said Henry sadly.

"What?"

"One might wonder how Bailey came to disappear, if your partner knew the tale. One might wonder if Bailey is alive? Is it not conceivable that Mr. Kaufman, placing all the blame on the other man, confronted his wife to tell her he had driven her lover away, even killed him, perhaps, and asked her to come back to him—and the response was suicide?"

"No," said Servais. "That is impossible."

"It would be best, then, to find Mr. Bailey and make sure he is alive. It is the one way of proving your partner's innocence. It may be a task for the police."

Servais had turned very pale. "I can't go to the police with a story like that."

"If you do not," said Henry, "it may be that your partner, brooding over what he has done—if indeed he has done it—will eventually take justice into his own hands."

"You mean kill himself?" whispered Servais. "Is that the choice you are facing me with: accuse him to the police or wait for him to kill himself?"

"Or both," said Henry. "Life is cruel."

THE BICENTENNIAL MAN

The Three Laws of Robotics:

1. *A robot may not injure a human being or, through inaction, allow a human being to come to harm.*
2. *A robot must obey the orders given it by human beings except where such orders would conflict with the First Law.*
3. *A robot must protect its own existence as long as such protection does not conflict with the First or Second Law.*

1.

Andrew Martin said, "Thank you," and took the seat offered him. He didn't look driven to the last resort, but he had been.

He didn't, actually, look anything, for there was a smooth blankness to his face, except for the sadness one imagined one saw in his eyes. His hair was smooth, light brown, rather fine, and there was no facial hair. He looked freshly and cleanly shaved. His clothes were distinctly old-fashioned, but neat and predominantly a velvety red-purple in color.

Facing him from behind the desk was the surgeon, and the nameplate on the desk included a fully identifying series of letters and numbers, which Andrew didn't bother with. To call him Doctor would be quite enough.

"When can the operation be carried through, Doctor?" he asked.

The surgeon said softly, with that certain inalienable note of respect that a robot always used to a human being, "I am not certain, sir, that I understand how or upon whom such an operation could be performed."

There might have been a look of respectful intransigence on the surgeon's face, if a robot of his sort, in lightly bronzed stainless steel, could have such an expression, or any expression.

Andrew Martin studied the robot's right hand, his cutting hand, as it lay on the desk in utter tranquillity. The fingers were long and shaped into artistically metallic looping curves so graceful and appropriate that one could imagine a scalpel fitting them and becoming, temporarily, one piece with them.

There would be no hesitation in his work, no stumbling, no quivering, no mistakes. That came with specialization, of course, a specialization so fiercely desired by humanity that few robots were, any longer, independently brained. A surgeon, of course, would have to be. And this one, though brained, was so limited in his capacity that he did not recognize Andrew—had probably never heard of him.

Andrew said, "Have you ever thought you would like to be a man?"

The surgeon hesitated a moment as though the question fitted nowhere in his allotted positronic pathways. "But I am a robot, sir."

"Would it be better to be a man?"

"It would be better, sir, to be a better surgeon. I could not be so if I were a man, but only if I were a more advanced robot. I would be pleased to be a more advanced robot."

"It does not offend you that I can order you about? That I can make you stand up, sit down, move right or left, by merely telling you to do so?"

"It is my pleasure to please you, sir. If your orders were to interfere with my functioning with respect to you or to any other human being, I would not obey you. The First Law, concerning my duty to human safety, would take precedence over the Second Law relating to obedience.

Otherwise, obedience is my pleasure . . . But upon whom am I to perform this operation?"

"Upon me," said Andrew.

"But that is impossible. It is patently a damaging operation."

"That does not matter," said Andrew calmly.

"I must not inflict damage," said the surgeon.

"On a human being, you must not," said Andrew, "but I, too, am a robot."

2.

Andrew had appeared much more a robot when he had first been—manufactured. He had then been as much a robot in appearance as any that had ever existed, smoothly designed and functional.

He had done well in the home to which he had been brought in those days when robots in households, or on the planet altogether, had been a rarity.

There had been four in the home: Sir and Ma'am and Miss and Little Miss. He knew their names, of course, but he never used them. Sir was Gerald Martin.

His own serial number was NDR—He forgot the numbers. It had been a long time, of course, but if he had wanted to remember, he could not forget. He had not wanted to remember.

Little Miss had been the first to call him Andrew because she could not use the letters, and all the rest followed her in this.

Little Miss— She had lived ninety years and was long since dead. He had tried to call her Ma'am once, but she would not allow it. Little Miss she had been to her last day.

Andrew had been intended to perform the duties of a valet, a butler, a lady's maid. Those were the experimental days for him and, indeed, for all robots anywhere but in the industrial and exploratory factories and stations off Earth.

The Martins enjoyed him, and half the time he was prevented from doing his work because Miss and Little Miss would rather play with him.

It was Miss who understood first how this might be arranged. She said, "We order you to play with us and you must follow orders."

Andrew said, "I am sorry, Miss, but a prior order from Sir must surely take precedence."

But she said, "Daddy just said he hoped you would take care of the cleaning. That's not much of an order. I *order* you."

Sir did not mind. Sir was fond of Miss and of Little Miss, even more than Ma'am was, and Andrew was fond of them, too. At least, the effect they had upon his actions were those which in a human being would have been called the result of fondness. Andrew thought of it as fondness, for he did not know any other word for it.

It was for Little Miss that Andrew had carved a pendant out of wood. She had ordered him to. Miss, it seemed, had received an ivorite pendant with scrollwork for her birthday and Little Miss was unhappy over it. She had only a piece of wood, which she gave Andrew together with a small kitchen knife.

He had done it quickly and Little Miss said, "That's *nice*, Andrew. I'll show it to Daddy."

Sir would not believe it. "Where did you really get this, Mandy?" Mandy was what he called Little Miss. When Little Miss assured him she was really telling the truth, he turned to Andrew. "Did you do this, Andrew?"

"Yes, Sir."

"The design, too?"

"Yes, Sir."

"From what did you copy the design?"

"It is a geometric representation, Sir, that fit the grain of the wood."

The next day, Sir brought him another piece of wood, a larger one, and an electric vibro-knife. He said, "Make something out of this, Andrew. Anything you want to."

Andrew did so and Sir watched, then looked at the product a long time. After that, Andrew no longer waited on tables. He was ordered to read books on furniture design instead, and he learned to make cabinets and desks.

Sir said, "These are amazing productions, Andrew."

Andrew said, "I enjoy doing them, Sir."

"Enjoy?"

"It makes the circuits of my brain somehow flow more easily. I have heard you use the word 'enjoy' and the way you use it fits the way I feel. I enjoy doing them, Sir."

3.

Gerald Martin took Andrew to the regional offices of United States Robots and Mechanical Men, Inc. As a member of the Regional Legislature he had no trouble at all in gaining an interview with the Chief Robopsychologist. In fact, it was only as a member of the Regional Legislature that he qualified as a robot owner in the first place—in those early days when robots were rare.

Andrew did not understand any of this at the time, but in later years, with greater learning, he could re-view that early scene and understand it in its proper light.

The robopsychologist, Merton Mansky, listened with a gathering frown and more than once managed to stop his fingers at the point beyond which they would have irrevocably drummed on the table. He had drawn features and a lined forehead and looked as though he might be younger than he looked.

He said, "Robotics is not an exact art, Mr. Martin. I cannot explain it to you in detail, but the mathematics governing the plotting of the positronic pathways is far too complicated to permit of any but approximate solutions. Naturally, since we build everything about the Three Laws, those are incontrovertible. We will, of course, replace your robot—"

"Not at all," said Sir. "There is no question of failure on his part. He performs his assigned duties perfectly. The point is, he also carves wood in exquisite fashion and never the same twice. He produces works of art."

Mansky looked confused. "Strange. Of course, we're attempting generalized pathways these days . . . Really creative, you think?"

"See for yourself." Sir handed over a little sphere of wood on which there was a playground scene in which the boys and girls were almost too small to make out, yet they were in perfect proportion and blended so naturally with the grain that that, too, seemed to have been carved.

Mansky said, "*He* did that?" He handed it back with a shake of his head. "The luck of the draw. Something in the pathways."

"Can you do it again?"

"Probably not. Nothing like this has ever been reported."

"Good! I don't in the least mind Andrew's being the only one."

Mansky said, "I suspect that the company would like to have your robot back for study."

Sir said with sudden grimness, "Not a chance. Forget it." He turned to Andrew, "Let's go home now."

"As you wish, Sir," said Andrew.

4.

Miss was dating boys and wasn't about the house much. It was Little Miss, not as little as she was, who filled Andrew's horizon now. She never forgot that the very first piece of wood carving he had done had been for her. She kept it on a silver chain about her neck.

It was she who first objected to Sir's habit of giving away the productions. She said, "Come on, Dad, if anyone wants one of them, let him pay for it. It's worth it."

Sir said, "It isn't like you to be greedy, Mandy."

"Not for us, Dad. For the artist."

Andrew had never heard the word before and when he had a moment to himself he looked it up in the dictionary. Then there was another trip, this time to Sir's lawyer.

Sir said to him, "What do you think of this, John?"

The lawyer was John Feingold. He had white hair and a pudgy belly, and the rims of his contact lenses were tinted a bright green. He looked at the small plaque Sir had given him. "This is beautiful . . . But I've heard the news. This is a carving made by your robot. The one you've brought with you."

"Yes, Andrew does them. Don't you, Andrew?"

"Yes, Sir," said Andrew.

"How much would you pay for that, John?" asked Sir.

"I can't say. I'm not a collector of such things."

"Would you believe I have been offered two hundred and fifty dollars for that small thing? Andrew has made chairs that have sold for five hundred dollars. There's two hundred thousand dollars in the bank out of Andrew's products."

"Good heavens, he's making you rich, Gerald."

"Half rich," said Sir. "Half of it is in an account in the name of Andrew Martin."

"The robot?"

"That's right, and I want to know if it's legal."

"Legal?" Feingold's chair creaked as he leaned back in it. "There are no precedents, Gerald. How did your robot sign the necessary papers?"

"He can sign his name and I brought in the signature. I didn't bring him in to the bank himself. Is there anything further that ought to be done?"

"Um." Feingold's eyes seemed to turn inward for a moment. Then he said, "Well, we can set up a trust to handle all finances in his name and that will place a layer of insulation between him and the hostile world. Further than that, my advice is you do nothing. No one is stopping you so far. If anyone objects, let *him* bring suit."

"And will you take the case if suit is brought?"

"For a retainer, certainly."

"How much?"

"Something like that," and Feingold pointed to the wooden plaque.

"Fair enough," said Sir.

Feingold chuckled as he turned to the robot. "Andrew, are you pleased that you have money?"

"Yes, sir."

"What do you plan to do with it?"

"Pay for things, sir, which otherwise Sir would have to pay for. It would save him expense, sir."

5.

The occasions came. Repairs were expensive, and revisions were even more so. With the years, new models of robots were produced and Sir saw to it that Andrew had the advantage of every new device until he was a paragon of metallic excellence. It was all at Andrew's expense.

Andrew insisted on that.

Only his positronic pathways were untouched. Sir insisted on that.

"The new ones aren't as good as you are, Andrew," he said. "The new robots are worthless. The company has learned to make the pathways more precise, more closely on the nose, more deeply on the track. The new robots don't shift. They do what they're designed for and never stray. I like you better."

"Thank you, Sir."

"And it's your doing, Andrew, don't you forget that. I am certain Mansky put an end to generalized pathways as soon as he had a good look at you. He didn't like the unpredictability . . . Do you know how many times he asked for you so he could place you under study? Nine times! I never let him have you, though, and now that he's retired, we may have some peace."

So Sir's hair thinned and grayed and his face grew pouchy, while Andrew looked rather better than he had when he first joined the family.

Ma'am had joined an art colony somewhere in Europe and Miss was a poet in New York. They wrote sometimes, but not often. Little Miss was married and lived not far away. She said she did not want to leave Andrew and when her child, Little Sir, was born, she let Andrew hold the bottle and feed him.

With the birth of a grandson, Andrew felt that Sir had someone now to replace those who had gone. It would not be so unfair to come to him with the request.

Andrew said, "Sir, it is kind of you to have allowed me to spend my money as I wished."

"It was your money, Andrew."

"Only by your voluntary act, Sir. I do not believe the law would have stopped you from keeping it all."

"The law won't persuade me to do wrong, Andrew."

"Despite all expenses, and despite taxes, too, Sir, I have nearly six hundred thousand dollars."

"I know that, Andrew."

"I want to give it to you, Sir."

"I won't take it, Andrew."

"In exchange for something you can give me, Sir."

"Oh? What is that, Andrew?"

"My freedom, Sir."

"Your—"

"I wish to buy my freedom, Sir."

6.

It wasn't that easy. Sir had flushed, had said "For God's sake!" had turned on his heel, and stalked away.

It was Little Miss who brought him around, defiantly and harshly—and in front of Andrew. For thirty years, no one had hesitated to talk in front of Andrew, whether the matter involved Andrew or not. He was only a robot.

She said, "Dad, why are you taking it as a personal affront? He'll still be here. He'll still be loyal. He can't help that. It's built in. All he wants is a form of words. He wants to be called free. Is that so terrible? Hasn't he earned it? Heavens, he and I have been talking about it for years."

"Talking about it for years, have you?"

"Yes, and over and over again, he postponed it for fear he would hurt you. I *made* him put it up to you."

"He doesn't know what freedom is. He's a robot."

"Dad, you don't know him. He's read everything in the library. I don't know what he feels inside but I don't know what *you* feel inside. When you talk to him you'll find he reacts to various abstractions as you and I do, and what else counts? If someone else's reactions are like your own, what more can you ask for?"

"The law won't take that attitude," Sir said angrily. "See here, you!" He turned to Andrew with a deliberate grate in his voice. "I can't free you except by doing it legally, and if it gets into the courts, you not only won't get your freedom but the law will take official cognizance of your money. They'll tell you that a robot has no right to earn money. Is this rigmarole worth losing your money?"

"Freedom is without price, Sir," said Andrew. "Even the chance of freedom is worth the money."

7.

The court might also take the attitude that freedom was without price, and might decide that for no price, however great, could a robot buy its freedom.

The simple statement of the regional attorney who represented those who had brought a class action to oppose the freedom was this: The word "freedom" had no meaning when applied to a robot. Only a human being could be free.

He said it several times, when it seemed appropriate; slowly, with his hand coming down rhythmically on the desk before him to mark the words.

Little Miss asked permission to speak on behalf of Andrew. She was recognized by her full name, something Andrew had never heard pronounced before:

"Amanda Laura Martin Charney may approach the bench."

She said, "Thank you, your honor. I am not a lawyer and I don't know the proper way of phrasing things, but I hope you will listen to my meaning and ignore the words.

"Let's understand what it means to be free in Andrew's case. In some ways, he *is* free. I think it's at least twenty years since anyone in the Martin family gave him an order to do something that we felt he might not do of his own accord.

"But we can, if we wish, give him an order to do anything, couch it as harshly as we wish, because he is a machine that belongs to us. Why should we be in a position to do so, when he has served us so long, so faithfully, and earned so much money for us? He owes us nothing more. The debt is entirely on the other side.

"Even if we were legally forbidden to place Andrew in involuntary servitude, he would still serve us voluntarily. Making him free would be a trick of words only, but it would mean much to him. It would give him everything and cost us nothing."

For a moment the Judge seemed to be suppressing a smile. "I see your point, Mrs. Charney. The fact is that there is no binding law in this respect and no precedent. There is, however, the unspoken assumption that only a man can enjoy freedom. I can make new law here, subject to reversal in a higher court, but I cannot lightly run counter to that assumption. Let me address the robot. Andrew!"

"Yes, your honor."

It was the first time Andrew had spoken in court and the Judge seemed astonished for a moment at the human timbre of the voice. He said, "Why do you want to be free, Andrew? In what way will this matter to you?"

Andrew said, "Would you wish to be a slave, your honor?"

"But you are not a slave. You are a perfectly good robot, a genius of a robot I am given to understand, capable of an artistic expression that can be matched nowhere. What more can you do if you were free?"

"Perhaps no more than I do now, your honor, but with greater joy. It has been said in this courtroom that only a human being can be free. It seems to me that only someone who wishes for freedom can be free. I wish for freedom."

And it was that that cued the Judge. The crucial sentence in his decision was: "There is no right to deny freedom to any object with a mind advanced enough to grasp the concept and desire the state."

It was eventually upheld by the World Court.

8.

Sir remained displeased and his harsh voice made Andrew feel almost as though he were being short-circuited.

Sir said, "I don't want your damned money, Andrew. I'll take it only because you won't feel free otherwise. From now on, you can select your own jobs and do them as you please. I will give you no orders, except this one—that you do as you please. But I am still responsible for you; that's part of the court order. I hope you understand that."

Little Miss interrupted. "Don't be irascible, Dad. The responsibility is no great chore. You know you won't have to do a thing. The Three Laws still hold."

"Then how is he free?"

Andrew said, "Are not human beings bound by their laws, Sir?"

Sir said, "I'm not going to argue." He left, and Andrew saw him only infrequently after that.

Little Miss came to see him frequently in the small house that had been built and made over for him. It had no kitchen, of course, nor bathroom facilities. It had just two rooms; one was a library and one was a combination storeroom and workroom. Andrew accepted many commissions and worked harder as a free robot than he ever had before, till the cost of the house was paid for and the structure legally transferred to him.

One day Little Sir came . . . No, George! Little Sir had insisted on that after the court decision. "A free robot doesn't call anyone Little Sir," George had said. "I call you Andrew. You must call me George."

It was phrased as an order, so Andrew called him George—but Little Miss remained Little Miss.

The day George came alone, it was to say that Sir was dying. Little Miss was at the bedside but Sir wanted Andrew as well.

Sir's voice was quite strong, though he seemed unable to move much. He struggled to get his hand up. "Andrew," he said, "Andrew— Don't help me, George. I'm only dying; I'm not crippled . . . Andrew, I'm glad you're free. I just wanted to tell you that."

Andrew did not know what to say. He had never been at the side of someone dying before, but he knew it was the human way of ceasing to function. It was an involuntary and irreversible dismantling, and Andrew did not know what to say that might be appropriate. He could only remain standing, absolutely silent, absolutely motionless.

When it was over, Little Miss said to him, "He may not have seemed friendly to you toward the end, Andrew, but he was old, you know, and it hurt him that you should want to be free."

And then Andrew found the words to say. He said, "I would never have been free without him, Little Miss."

9.

It was only after Sir's death that Andrew began to wear clothes. He began with an old pair of trousers at first, a pair that George had given him.

George was married now, and a lawyer. He had joined Feingold's firm. Old Feingold was long since dead but his daughter had carried on and eventually the firm's name became Feingold and Martin. It remained so even when the daughter retired and no Feingold took her place. At the time Andrew put on clothes for the first time, the Martin name had just been added to the firm.

George had tried not to smile, the first time Andrew put on the trousers, but to Andrew's eyes the smile was clearly there.

George showed Andrew how to manipulate the static charge so as to allow the trousers to open, wrap about his lower body, and move shut. George demonstrated on his own trousers, but Andrew was quite aware that it would take him awhile to duplicate that one flowing motion.

George said, "But why do you want trousers, Andrew? Your body is so beautifully functional it's a shame to cover it—especially when you needn't worry about either temperature control or modesty. And it doesn't cling properly, not on metal."

Andrew said, "Are not human bodies beautifully functional, George? Yet you cover yourselves."

"For warmth, for cleanliness, for protection, for decorativeness. None of that applies to you."

Andrew said, "I feel bare without clothes. I feel different, George."

"Different! Andrew, there are millions of robots on Earth now. In this region, according to the last census, there are almost as many robots as there are men."

"I know, George. There are robots doing every conceivable type of work."

"And none of them wear clothes."

"But none of them are free, George."

Little by little, Andrew added to the wardrobe. He was inhibited by George's smile and by the stares of the people who commissioned work.

He might be free, but there was built into him a carefully detailed program concerning his behavior toward people, and it was only by the tiniest steps that he dared advance. Open disapproval would set him back months.

Not everyone accepted Andrew as free. He was incapable of resenting that and yet there was a difficulty about his thinking process when he thought of it.

Most of all, he tended to avoid putting on clothes—or too many of them—when he thought Little Miss might come to visit him. She was old now and was often away in some warmer climate, but when she returned the first thing she did was visit him.

On one of her returns, George said ruefully, "She's got me, Andrew. I'll be running for the Legislature next year. Like grandfather, she says, like grandson."

"Like grandfather—" Andrew stopped, uncertain.

"I mean that I, George, the grandson, will be like Sir, the grandfather, who was in the Legislature once."

Andrew said, "It would be pleasant, George, if Sir were still—" He paused, for he did not want to say, "in working order." That seemed inappropriate.

"Alive," said George. "Yes, I think of the old monster now and then, too."

It was a conversation Andrew thought about. He had noticed his own incapacity in speech when talking with George. Somehow the language had changed since Andrew had come into being with an innate vocabulary. Then, too, George used a colloquial speech, as Sir and Little Miss had not. Why should he have called Sir a monster when surely that word was not appropriate?

Nor could Andrew turn to his own books for guidance. They were old and most dealt with woodworking, with art, with furniture design. There were none on language, none on the way of human beings.

It was at that moment it seemed to him that he must seek the proper books; and as a free robot, he felt he must not ask George. He would go to town and use the library. It was a triumphant decision and he felt his electropotential grow distinctly higher until he had to throw in an impedance coil.

He put on a full costume, even including a shoulder chain of wood. He would have preferred the glitter plastic but George had said that wood was much more appropriate and that polished cedar was considerably more valuable as well.

He had placed a hundred feet between himself and the house before gathering resistance brought him to a halt. He shifted the impedance coil out of circuit, and when that did not seem to help enough, he returned to his home and on a piece of notepaper wrote neatly, "I have gone to the library," and placed it in clear view on his worktable.

10.

Andrew never quite got to the library. He had studied the map. He knew the route, but not the appearance of it. The actual landmarks did not resemble the symbols on the map and he would hesitate. Eventually he thought he must have somehow gone wrong, for everything looked strange.

He passed an occasional field robot, but at the time he decided he should ask his way, there were none in sight. A vehicle passed and did not stop. He stood irresolute, which meant calmly motionless, and then coming across the field toward him were two human beings.

He turned to face them, and they altered their course to meet him. A moment before, they had been talking loudly; he had heard their voices; but now they were silent. They had the look that Andrew associated with human uncertainty, and they were young, but not very young. Twenty perhaps? Andrew could never judge human age.

He said, "Would you describe to me the route to the town library, sirs?"

One of them, the taller of the two, whose tall hat

lengthened him still farther, almost grotesquely, said, not to Andrew, but to the other, "It's a robot."

The other had a bulbous nose and heavy eyelids. He said, not to Andrew, but to the first, "It's wearing clothes."

The tall one snapped his fingers. "It's the free robot. They have a robot at the Martins who isn't owned by anybody. Why else would it be wearing clothes?"

"Ask it," said the one with the nose.

"Are you the Martin robot?" asked the tall one.

"I am Andrew Martin, sir," said Andrew.

"Good. Take off your clothes. Robots don't wear clothes." He said to the other, "That's disgusting. Look at him."

Andrew hesitated. He hadn't heard an order in that tone of voice in so long that his Second Law circuits had momentarily jammed.

The tall one said, "Take off your clothes. I order you."

Slowly, Andrew began to remove them.

"Just drop them," said the tall one.

The nose said, "If it doesn't belong to anyone, he could be ours as much as someone else's."

"Anyway," said the tall one, "who's to object to anything we do? We're not damaging property . . . Stand on your head." That was to Andrew.

"The head is not meant—" began Andrew.

"That's an order. If you don't know how, try anyway."

Andrew hesitated again, then bent to put his head on the ground. He tried to lift his legs and fell, heavily.

The tall one said, "Just lie there." He said to the other, "We can take him apart. Ever take a robot apart?"

"Will he let us?"

"How can he stop us?"

There was no way Andrew could stop them, if they ordered him not to resist in a forceful enough manner. Second Law of obedience took precedence over the Third Law of self-preservation. In any case, he could not defend himself without possibly hurting them and that would mean breaking the First Law. At that thought, every motile unit contracted slightly and he quivered as he lay there.

The tall one walked over and pushed at him with his foot. "He's heavy. I think we'll need tools to do the job."

The nose said, "We could order him to take himself apart. It would be fun to watch him try."

"Yes," said the tall one thoughtfully, "but let's get him off the road. If someone comes along—"

It was too late. Someone had indeed come along and it was George. From where he lay, Andrew had seen him topping a small rise in the middle distance. He would have liked to signal him in some way, but the last order had been "Just lie there!"

George was running now and he arrived somewhat winded. The two young men stepped back a little and then waited thoughtfully.

George said anxiously, "Andrew, has something gone wrong?"

Andrew said, "I am well, George."

"Then stand up . . . What happened to your clothes?"

The tall man said, "That your robot, mac?"

George turned sharply. "He's no one's robot. What's been going on here?"

"We politely asked him to take his clothes off. What's that to you if you don't own him?"

George said, "What were they doing, Andrew?"

Andrew said, "It was their intention in some way to dismember me. They were about to move me to a quiet spot and order me to dismember myself."

George looked at the two and his chin trembled. The two young men retreated no further. They were smiling. The tall one said lightly, "What are you going to do, pudgy? Attack us?"

George said, "No. I don't have to. This robot has been

with my family for over seventy years. He knows us and he values us more than he values anyone else. I am going to tell him that you two are threatening my life and that you plan to kill me. I will ask him to defend me. In choosing between me and you two, he will choose me. Do you know what will happen to you when he attacks you?"

The two were backing away slightly, looking uneasy.

George said sharply, "Andrew, I am in danger and about to come to harm from these young men. Move toward them!"

Andrew did so, and the two young men did not wait. They ran fleetly.

"All right, Andrew, relax," said George. He looked unstrung. He was far past the age where he could face the possibility of a dustup with one young man, let alone two.

Andrew said, "I couldn't have hurt them, George. I could see they were not attacking you."

"I didn't order you to attack them; I only told you to move toward them. Their own fears did the rest."

"How can they fear robots?"

"It's a disease of mankind, one of which it is not yet cured. But never mind that. What the devil are you doing here, Andrew? I was on the point of turning back and hiring a helicopter when I found you. How did you get it into your head to go to the library? I would have brought you any books you needed."

"I am a—" began Andrew.

"Free robot. Yes, yes. All right, what did you want in the library?"

"I want to know more about human beings, about the world, about everything. And about robots, George. I want to write a history about robots."

George said, "Well, let's walk home . . . And pick up your clothes first. Andrew, there are a million books on robotics and all of them include histories of the science. The world is growing saturated not only with robots but with information about robots."

Andrew shook his head, a human gesture he had lately begun to make. "Not a history of robotics, George. A history of *robots*, by a robot. I want to explain how robots feel about what has happened since the first ones were allowed to work and live on Earth."

George's eyebrows lifted, but he said nothing in direct response.

11.

Little Miss was just past her eighty-third birthday, but there was nothing about her that was lacking in either energy or determination. She gestured with her cane oftener than she propped herself up with it.

She listened to the story in a fury of indignation. She said, "George, that's horrible. Who were those young ruffians?"

"I don't know. What difference does it make? In the end they did no damage."

"They might have. You're a lawyer, George, and if you're well off, it's entirely due to the talent of Andrew. It was the money *he* earned that is the foundation of everything we have. He provides the continuity for this family and I will *not* have him treated as a wind-up toy."

"What would you have me do, Mother?" asked George.

"I said you're a lawyer. Don't you listen? You set up a test case somehow, and you force the regional courts to declare for robot rights and get the Legislature to pass the necessary bills, and carry the whole thing to the World Court, if you have to. I'll be watching, George, and I'll tolerate no shirking."

She was serious, and what began as a way of soothing the

fearsome old lady became an involved matter with enough legal entanglement to make it interesting. As senior partner of Feingold and Martin, George plotted strategy but left the actual work to his junior partners, with much of it a matter for his son, Paul, who was also a member of the firm and who reported dutifully nearly every day to his grandmother. She, in turn, discussed it every day with Andrew.

Andrew was deeply involved. His work on his book on robots was delayed again, as he pored over the legal arguments and even, at times, made very diffident suggestions.

He said, "George told me that day that human beings have always been afraid of robots. As long as they are, the courts and the legislatures are not likely to work hard on behalf of robots. Should there not be something done about public opinion?"

So while Paul stayed in court, George took to the public platform. It gave him the advantage of being informal and he even went so far sometimes as to wear the new, loose style of clothing which he called drapery. Paul said, "Just don't trip over it on stage, Dad."

George said despondently, "I'll try not to."

He addressed the annual convention of holo-news editors on one occasion and said, in part:

"If, by virtue of the Second Law, we can demand of any robot unlimited obedience in all respects not involving harm to a human being, then any human being, *any* human being, has a fearsome power over any robot, *any* robot. In particular, since Second Law supersedes Third Law, *any* human being can use the law of obedience to overcome the law of self-protection. He can order any robot to damage itself or even destroy itself for any reason, or for no reason.

"Is this just? Would we treat an animal so? Even an inanimate object which has given us good service has a claim on our consideration. And a robot is not insensible; it is not an animal. It can think well enough to enable it to talk to us, reason with us, joke with us. Can we treat them as friends, can we work together with them, and not give them some of the fruit of that friendship, some of the benefit of co-working?

"If a man has the right to give a robot any order that does not involve harm to a human being, he should have the decency never to give a robot any order that involves harm to a robot, unless human safety absolutely requires it. With great power goes great responsibility, and if the robots have Three Laws to protect men, is it too much to ask that men have a law or two to protect robots?"

Andrew was right. It was the battle over public opinion that held the key to courts and Legislature and in the end a law passed which set up conditions under which robot-harming orders were forbidden. It was endlessly qualified and the punishments for violating the law were totally inadequate, but the principle was established. The final passage by the World Legislature came through on the day of Little Miss's death.

That was no coincidence. Little Miss held on to life desperately during the last debate and let go only when word of victory arrived. Her last smile was for Andrew. Her last words were: "You have been good to us, Andrew."

She died with her hand holding his, while her son and his wife and children remained at a respectful distance from both.

12.

Andrew waited patiently while the receptionist disappeared into the inner office. It might have used the holographic chatterbox, but unquestionably it was unmanned (or perhaps unroboted) by having to deal with another robot rather than with a human being.

Andrew passed the time revolving the matter in his mind. Could "unroboted" be used as an analogue of "unmanned," or had "unmanned" become a metaphoric term sufficiently divorced from its original literal meaning to be applied to robots—or to women for that matter?

Such problems came frequently as he worked on his book on robots. The trick of thinking out sentences to express all complexities had undoubtedly increased his vocabulary.

Occasionally, someone came into the room to stare at him and he did not try to avoid the glance. He looked at each calmly, and each in turn looked away.

Paul Martin finally came out. He looked surprised, or he would have if Andrew could have made out his expression with certainty. Paul had taken to wearing the heavy makeup that fashion was dictating for both sexes and though it made sharper and firmer the somewhat bland lines of his face, Andrew disapproved. He found that disapproving of human beings, as long as he did not express it verbally, did not make him very uneasy. He could even write the disapproval. He was sure it had not always been so.

Paul said, "Come in, Andrew. I'm sorry I made you wait but there was something I *had* to finish. Come in. You had said you wanted to talk to me, but I didn't know you meant here in town."

"If you are busy, Paul, I am prepared to continue to wait."

Paul glanced at the interplay of shifting shadows on the dial on the wall that served as timepiece and said, "I can make some time. Did you come alone?"

"I hired an automatobile."

"Any trouble?" Paul asked, with more than a trace of anxiety.

"I wasn't expecting any. My rights are protected."

Paul looked the more anxious for that. "Andrew, I've explained that the law is unenforceable, at least under most conditions . . . And if you insist on wearing clothes, you'll run into trouble eventually . . . just like that first time."

"And only time, Paul. I'm sorry you are displeased."

"Well, look at it this way; you are virtually a living legend, Andrew, and you are too valuable in many different ways for you to have any right to take chances with yourself . . . How's the book coming?"

"I am approaching the end, Paul. The publisher is quite pleased."

"Good!"

"I don't know that he's necessarily pleased with the book as a book. I think he expects to sell many copies because it's written by a robot and it's that that pleases him."

"Only human, I'm afraid."

"I am not displeased. Let it sell for whatever reason since it will mean money and I can use some."

"Grandmother left you—"

"Little Miss was generous, and I'm sure I can count on the family to help me out further. But it is the royalties from the book on which I am counting to help me through the next step."

"What next step is that?"

"I wish to see the head of U. S. Robots and Mechanical Men, Inc. I have tried to make an appointment, but so far I have not been able to reach him. The corporation did not cooperate with me in the writing of the book, so I am not surprised, you understand."

Paul was clearly amused. "Cooperation is the last thing you can expect. They didn't cooperate with us in our great fight for robot rights. Quite the reverse and you can see why. Give a robot rights and people may not want to buy them."

"Nevertheless," said Andrew, "if you call them, you may obtain an interview for me."

"I'm no more popular with them than you are, Andrew."

"But perhaps you can hint that by seeing me they may head off a campaign by Feingold and Martin to strengthen the rights of robots further."

"Wouldn't that be a lie, Andrew?"

"Yes, Paul, and I can't tell one. That is why you must call."

"Ah, you can't lie, but you can urge me to tell a lie, is that it? You're getting more human all the time, Andrew."

13.

It was not easy to arrange, even with Paul's supposedly weighted name.

But it was finally carried through and, when it was, Harley Smythe-Robertson, who, on his mother's side, was descended from the original founder of the corporation and who had adopted the hyphenation to indicate it, looked remarkably unhappy. He was approaching retirement age and his entire tenure as president had been devoted to the matter of robot rights. His gray hair was plastered thinly over the top of his scalp, his face was not made up, and he eyed Andrew with brief hostility from time to time.

Andrew said, "Sir, nearly a century ago, I was told by a Merton Mansky of this corporation that the mathematics governing the plotting of the positronic pathways was far too complicated to permit of any but approximate solutions and that therefore my own capacities were not fully predictable."

"That was a century ago." Smythe-Robertson hesitated, then said icily, "*Sir*. It is true no longer. Our robots are made with precision now and are trained precisely to their jobs."

"Yes," said Paul, who had come along, as he said, to make sure that the corporation played fair, "with the result that my receptionist must be guided at every point once events depart from the conventional, however slightly."

Smythe-Robertson said, "You would be much more displeased if it were to improvise."

Andrew said, "Then you no longer manufacture robots like myself which are flexible and adaptable."

"No longer."

"The research I have done in connection with my book," said Andrew, "indicates that I am the oldest robot presently in active operation."

"The oldest presently," said Smythe-Robertson, "and the oldest ever. The oldest that will ever be. No robot is useful after the twenty-fifth year. They are called in and replaced with newer models."

"No robot *as presently manufactured* is useful after the twenty-fifth year," said Paul pleasantly. "Andrew is quite exceptional in this respect."

Andrew, adhering to the path he had marked out for himself, said, "As the oldest robot in the world and the most flexible, am I not unusual enough to merit special treatment from the company?"

"Not at all," said Smythe-Robertson freezingly. "Your unusualness is an embarrassment to the company. If you were on lease, instead of having been a sale outright through some mischance, you would long since have been replaced."

"But that is exactly the point," said Andrew. "I am a free robot and I own myself. Therefore I come to you and ask you to replace me. You cannot do this without the owner's consent. Nowadays, that consent is extorted as a condition of the lease, but in my time this did not happen."

Smythe-Robertson was looking both startled and puzzled, and for a moment there was silence. Andrew found himself staring at the holograph on the wall. It was a death mask of Susan Calvin, patron saint of all roboticists. She was dead nearly two centuries now, but as a result of writing this book Andrew knew her so well he could half persuade himself that he had met her in life.

Smythe-Robertson said, "How can I replace you for you? If I replace you as robot, how can I donate the new robot to you as owner since in the very act of replacement you cease to exist?" He smiled grimly.

"Not at all difficult," interposed Paul. "The seat of Andrew's personality is his positronic brain and it is the one part that cannot be replaced without creating a new robot. The positronic brain, therefore, is Andrew the owner. Every other part of the robotic body can be replaced without affecting the robot's personality, and those other parts are the brain's possessions. Andrew, I should say, wants to supply his brain with a new robotic body."

"That's right," said Andrew calmly. He turned to Smythe-Robertson. "You have manufactured androids, haven't you? Robots that have the outward appearance of humans complete to the texture of the skin?"

Smythe-Robertson said, "Yes, we have. They worked perfectly well, with their synthetic fibrous skins and tendons. There was virtually no metal anywhere except for the brain, yet they were nearly as tough as metal robots. They were tougher, weight for weight."

Paul looked interested. "I didn't know that. How many are on the market?"

"None," said Smythe-Robertson. "They were much more expensive than metal models and a market survey showed they would not be accepted. They looked too human."

Andrew said, "But the corporation retains its expertise, I

assume. Since it does, I wish to request that I be replaced by an organic robot, an android."

Paul looked surprised. "Good Lord," he said.

Smythe-Robertson stiffened. "Quite impossible!"

"Why is it impossible?" asked Andrew. "I will pay any reasonable fee, of course.

Smythe-Robertson said, "We do not manufacture androids."

"You do not *choose* to manufacture androids," interposed Paul quickly. "That is not the same as being unable to manufacture them."

Smythe-Robertson said, "Nevertheless, the manufacture of androids is against public policy."

"There is no law against it," said Paul.

"Nevertheless, we do not manufacture them, and we will not."

Paul cleared his throat. "Mr. Smythe-Robertson," he said, "Andrew is a free robot who is under the purview of the law guaranteeing robot rights. You are aware of this, I take it?"

"Only too well."

"This robot, as a free robot, chooses to wear clothes. This results in his being frequently humiliated by thoughtless human beings despite the law against the humiliation of robots. It is difficult to prosecute vague offenses that don't meet with the general disapproval of those who must decide on guilt and innocence."

"U. S. Robots understood that from the start. Your father's firm unfortunately did not."

"My father is dead now," said Paul, "but what I see is that we have here a clear offense with a clear target."

"What are you talking about?" said Smythe-Robertson.

"My client, Andrew Martin—he has just become my client—is a free robot who is entitled to ask U. S. Robots and Mechanical Men, Inc., for the right of replacement, which the corporation supplies anyone who owns a robot for more than twenty-five years. In fact, the corporation insists on such replacement."

Paul was smiling and thoroughly at his ease. He went on, "The positronic brain of my client is the owner of the body of my client—which is certainly more than twenty-five years old. The positronic brain demands the replacement of the body and offers to pay any reasonable fee for an android body as that replacement. If you refuse the request, my client undergoes humiliation and we will sue.

"While public opinion would not ordinarily support the claim of a robot in such a case, may I remind you that U. S. Robots is not popular with the public generally. Even those who most use and profit from robots are suspicious of the corporation. This may be a hangover from the days when robots were widely feared. It may be resentment against the power and wealth of U. S. Robots which has a worldwide monopoly. Whatever the cause may be, the resentment exists and I think you will find that you would prefer not to withstand a lawsuit, particularly since my client is wealthy and will live for many more centuries and will have no reason to refrain from fighting the battle forever."

Smythe-Robertson had slowly reddened. "You are trying to force me to . . ."

"I force you to do nothing," said Paul. "If you wish to refuse to accede to my client's reasonable request, you may by all means do so and we will leave without another word . . . But we will sue, as is certainly our right, and you will find that you will eventually lose."

Smythe-Robertson said, "Well—" and paused.

"I see that you are going to accede," said Paul. "You may hesitate but you will come to it in the end. Let me assure you, then, of one further point. If, in the process of transferring my client's positronic brain from his present body to an organic one, there is any damage, however slight, then I will never rest till I've nailed the corporation to the ground. I will, if necessary, take every possible step to mobilize public opinion against the corporation if one brain path of my client's platinum-iridium essence is scrambled." He turned to Andrew and said, "Do you agree to all this, Andrew?"

Andrew hesitated a full minute. It amounted to the approval of lying, of blackmail, of the badgering and humiliation of a human being. But not physical harm, he told himself, not physical harm.

He managed at last to come out with a rather faint "Yes."

14.

It was like being constructed again. For days, then for weeks, finally for months, Andrew found himself not himself somehow, and the simplest actions kept giving rise to hesitation.

Paul was frantic. "They've damaged you, Andrew. We'll have to institute suit."

Andrew spoke very slowly. "You mustn't. You'll never be able to prove—something—m-m-m-m—"

"Malice?"

"Malice. Besides, I grow stronger, better. It's the tr-tr-tr—"

"Tremble?"

"Trauma. After all, there's never been such an op—op—op—before."

Andrew could feel his brain from the inside. No one else could. He knew he was well and during the months that it took him to learn full coordination and full positronic interplay, he spent hours before the mirror.

Not quite human! The face was stiff—too stiff—and the motions were too deliberate. They lacked the careless free flow of the human being, but perhaps that might come with time. At least he could wear clothes without the ridiculous anomaly of a metal face going along with it.

Eventually he said, "I will be going back to work."

Paul laughed and said, "That means you are well. What will you be doing? Another book?"

"No," said Andrew seriously. "I live too long for any career to seize me by the throat and never let me go. There was a time when I was primarily an artist and I can still turn to that. And there was a time when I was a historian and I can still turn to that. But now I wish to be a robobiologist."

"A robopsychologist, you mean."

"No. That would imply the study of positronic brains and at the moment I lack the desire to do that. A robobiologist, it seems to me, would be concerned with the working of the body attached to that brain."

"Wouldn't that be a roboticist?"

"A roboticist works with a metal body. I would be studying an organic humanoid body, of which I have the only one, as far as I know."

"You narrow your field," said Paul thoughtfully. "As an artist, all conception is yours; as a historian, you dealt chiefly with robots; as a robobiologist, you will deal with yourself."

Andrew nodded. "It would seem so."

Andrew had to start from the very beginning, for he knew nothing of ordinary biology, almost nothing of science. He became a familiar sight in the libraries, where he sat at the electronic indices for hours at a time, looking perfectly normal in clothes. Those few who knew he was a robot in no way interfered with him.

He built a laboratory in a room which he added to his house, and his library grew, too.

Years passed, and Paul came to him one day and said, "It's a pity you're no longer working on the history of robots. I understand U. S. Robots is adopting a radically new policy."

Paul had aged, and his deteriorating eyes had been replaced with photoptic cells. In that respect, he had drawn closer to Andrew. Andrew said, "What have they done?"

"They are manufacturing central computers, gigantic positronic brains, really, which communicate with anywhere from a dozen to a thousand robots by microwave. The robots themselves have no brains at all. They are the limbs of the gigantic brain, and the two are physically separate."

"Is that more efficient?"

"U. S. Robots claims it is. Smythe-Robertson established the new direction before he died, however, and it's my notion that it's a backlash at you. U. S. Robots is determined that they will make no robots that will give them the type of trouble you have, and for that reason they separate brain and body. The brain will have no body to wish changed; the body will have no brain to wish anything.

"It's amazing, Andrew," Paul went on, "the influence you have had on the history of robots. It was your artistry that encouraged U. S. Robots to make robots more precise and specialized; it was your freedom that resulted in the establishment of the principle of robotic rights; it was your insistence on an android body that made U. S. Robots switch to brain-body separation."

Andrew said, "I suppose in the end the corporation will produce one vast brain controlling several billion robotic bodies. All the eggs will be in one basket. Dangerous. Not proper at all."

"I think you're right," said Paul, "but I don't suspect it will come to pass for a century at least and I won't live to see it. In fact, I may not live to see next year."

"Paul!" said Andrew, in concern.

Paul shrugged. "We're mortal, Andrew. We're not like

you. It doesn't matter too much, but it does make it important to assure you on one point. I'm the last of the human Martins. There are collaterals descended from my great-aunt, but they don't count. The money I control personally will be left to the trust in your name and as far as anyone can foresee the future, you will be economically secure."

"Unnecessary," said Andrew, with difficulty. In all this time, he could not get used to the deaths of the Martins.

Paul said, "Let's not argue. That's the way it's going to be. What are you working on?"

"I am designing a system for allowing androids—myself—to gain energy from the combustion of hydrocarbons, rather than from atomic cells."

Paul raised his eyebrows. "So that they will breathe and eat?"

"Yes."

"How long have you been pushing in that direction?"

"For a long time now, but I think I have designed an adequate combustion chamber for catalyzed controlled breakdown."

"But why, Andrew? The atomic cell is surely infinitely better."

"In some ways, perhaps, but the atomic cell is inhuman."

15.

It took time, but Andrew had time. In the first place, he did not wish to do anything till Paul had died in peace.

With the death of the great-grandson of Sir, Andrew felt more nearly exposed to a hostile world and for that reason was the more determined to continue the path he had long ago chosen.

Yet he was not really alone. If a man had died, the firm

of Feingold and Martin lived, for a corporation does not die any more than a robot does. The firm had its directions and it followed them soullessly. By the way of the trust and through the law firm, Andrew continued to be wealthy. And in return for their own large annual retainer, Feingold and Martin involved themselves in the legal aspects of the new combustion chamber.

When the time came for Andrew to visit U. S. Robots and Mechanical Men, Inc., he did it alone. Once he had gone with Sir and once with Paul. This time, the third time, he was alone and manlike.

U. S. Robots had changed. The production plant had been shifted to a large space station, as had grown to be the case with more and more industries. With them had gone many robots. The Earth itself was becoming parklike, with its one-billion-person population stabilized and perhaps not more than thirty per cent of its at least equally large robot population independently brained.

The Director of Research was Alvin Magdescu, dark of complexion and hair, with a little pointed beard and wearing nothing above the waist but the breastband that fashion dictated. Andrew himself was well covered in the older fashion of several decades back.

Magdescu said, "I know you, of course, and I'm rather pleased to see you. You're our most notorious product and it's a pity old Smythe-Robertson was so set against you. We could have done a great deal with you."

"You still can," said Andrew.

"No, I don't think so. We're past the time. We've had robots on Earth for over a century, but that's changing. It will be back to space with them and those that stay here won't be brained."

"But there remains myself, and I stay on Earth."

"True, but there doesn't seem to be much of the robot about you. What new request have you?"

"To be still less a robot. Since I am so far organic, I wish an organic source of energy. I have here the plans—"

Magdescu did not hasten through them. He might have intended to at first, but he stiffened and grew intent. At one point he said, "This is remarkably ingenious. Who thought of all this?"

"I did," said Andrew.

Magdescu looked up at him sharply, then said, "It would amount to a major overhaul of your body, and an experimental one, since it has never been attempted before. I advise against it. Remain as you are."

Andrew's face had limited means of expression, but impatience showed plainly in his voice. "Dr. Magdescu, you miss the entire point. You have no choice but to accede to my request. If such devices can be built into my body, they can be built into human bodies as well. The tendency to lengthen human life by prosthetic devices has already been remarked on. There are no devices better than the ones I have designed and am designing.

"As it happens, I control the patents by way of the firm of Feingold and Martin. We are quite capable of going into business for ourselves and of developing the kind of prosthetic devices that may end by producing human beings with many of the properties of robots. Your own business will then suffer.

"If, however, you operate on me now and agree to do so under similar circumstances in the future, you will receive permission to make use of the patents and control the technology of both robots and the prosthetization of human beings. The initial leasing will not be granted, of course, until after the first operation is completed successfully, and after enough time has passed to demonstrate that it is indeed successful." Andrew felt scarcely any First Law inhibition to the stern conditions he was setting a human being. He was learning to reason that what seemed like cruelty might, in the long run, be kindness.

Magdescu looked stunned. He said, "I'm not the one to decide something like this. That's a corporate decision that would take time."

"I can wait a reasonable time," said Andrew, "but only a reasonable time." And he thought with satisfaction that Paul himself could not have done it better.

16.

It took only a reasonable time, and the operation was a success.

Magdescu said, "I was very much against the operation, Andrew, but not for the reasons you might think. I was not in the least against the experiment, if it had been on someone else. I hated risking *your* positronic brain. Now that you have the positronic pathways interacting with simulated nerve pathways, it might be difficult to rescue the brain intact if the body went bad."

"I had every faith in the skill of the staff at U. S. Robots," said Andrew. "And I can eat now."

"Well, you can sip olive oil. It will mean occasional cleanings of the combustion chamber, as we have explained to you. Rather an uncomfortable touch, I should think."

"Perhaps, if I did not expect to go further. Self-cleaning is not impossible. In fact, I am working on a device that will deal with solid food that may be expected to contain incombustible fractions—indigestible matter, so to speak, that will have to be discarded."

"You would then have to develop an anus."

"The equivalent."

"What else, Andrew?"

"Everything else."

"Genitalia, too?"

"Insofar as they will fit my plans. My body is a canvas on which I intend to draw—"

Magdescu waited for the sentence to be completed, and when it seemed that it would not be, he completed it himself. "A man?"

"We shall see," said Andrew.

Magdescu said, "It's a puny ambition, Andrew. You're better than a man. You've gone downhill from the moment you opted for organicism."

"My brain has not suffered."

"No, it hasn't. I'll grant you that. But, Andrew, the whole new breakthrough in prosthetic devices made possible by your patents is being marketed under your name. You're recognized as the inventor and you're honored for it—as you are. Why play further games with your body?"

Andrew did not answer.

The honors came. He accepted membership in several learned societies, including one which was devoted to the new science he had established; the one he had called robobiology but had come to be termed prosthetology.

On the one hundred and fiftieth anniversary of his construction, there was a testimonial dinner given in his honor at U. S. Robots. If Andrew saw irony in this, he kept it to himself.

Alvin Magdescu came out of retirement to chair the dinner. He was himself ninety-four years old and was alive because he had prosthetized devices that, among other things, fulfilled the function of liver and kidneys. The dinner reached its climax when Magdescu, after a short and emotional talk, raised his glass to toast "the Sesquicentennial Robot."

Andrew had had the sinews of his face redesigned to the point where he could show a range of emotions, but he sat through all the ceremonies solemnly passive. He did not like to be a Sesquicentennial Robot.

17.

It was prosthetology that finally took Andrew off the Earth. In the decades that followed the celebration of the Sesquicentennial, the Moon had come to be a world more Earth-like than Earth in every respect but its gravitational pull and in its underground cities there was a fairly dense population.

Prosthetized devices there had to take the lesser gravity into account and Andrew spent five years on the Moon working with local prosthetologists to make the necessary adaptations. When not at his work, he wandered among the robot population, every one of which treated him with the robotic obsequiousness due a man.

He came back to an Earth that was humdrum and quiet in comparison and visited the offices of Feingold and Martin to announce his return.

The current head of the firm, Simon DeLong, was surprised. He said, "We had been told you were returning, Andrew" (he had almost said "Mr. Martin"), "but we were not expecting you till next week."

"I grew impatient," said Andrew brusquely. He was anxious to get to the point. "On the Moon, Simon, I was in charge of research team of twenty human scientists. I gave orders that no one questioned. The Lunar robots deferred to me as they would to a human being. Why, then, am I not a human being?"

A wary look entered DeLong's eyes. He said, "My dear Andrew, as you have just explained, you are treated as a human being by both robots and human beings. You are therefore a human being *de facto*."

"To be a human being *de facto* is not enough. I want not only to be treated as one, but to be legally identified as one. I want to be a human being *de jure*."

"Now that is another matter," said DeLong. "There we would run into human prejudice and into the undoubted fact that however much you may be like a human being, you are *not* a human being."

"In what way not?" asked Andrew. "I have the shape of a human being and organs equivalent to those of a human being. My organs, in fact, are identical to some of those in a prosthetized human being. I have contributed artistically, literarily, and scientifically to human culture as much as any human being now alive. What more can one ask?"

"I myself would ask nothing more. The trouble is that it would take an act of the World Legislature to define you as a human being. Frankly, I wouldn't expect that to happen."

"To whom on the Legislature could I speak?"

"To the chairman of the Science and Technology Committee perhaps."

"Can you arrange a meeting?"

"But you scarcely need an intermediary. In your position, you can—"

"No. *You* arrange it." (It didn't even occur to Andrew that he was giving a flat order to a human being. He had grown accustomed to that on the Moon.) "I want him to know that the firm of Feingold and Martin is backing me in this to the hilt."

"Well, now—"

"To the hilt, Simon. In one hundred and seventy-three years I have in one fashion or another contributed greatly to this firm. I have been under obligation to individual members of the firm in times past. I am not now. It is rather the other way around now and I am calling in my debts."

DeLong said, "I will do what I can."

18.

The chairman of the Science and Technology Committee was of the East Asian region and she was a woman. Her name was Chee Li-Hsing and her transparent garments (obscuring what she wanted obscured only by their dazzle) made her look plastic-wrapped.

She said, "I sympathize with your wish for full human rights. There have been times in history when segments of the human population fought for full human rights. What rights, however, can you possibly want that you did not have?"

"As simple a thing as my right to life. A robot can be dismantled at any time."

"A human being can be executed at any time."

"Execution can only follow due process of law. There is no trial needed for my dismantling. Only the word of a human being in authority is needed to end me. Besides— besides—" Andrew tried desperately to allow no sign of pleading, but his carefully designed tricks of human expression and tone of voice betrayed him here. "The truth is, I want to be a man. I have wanted it through six generations of human beings."

Li-Hsing looked up at him out of darkly sympathetic eyes. "The Legislature can pass a law declaring you one—they could pass a law declaring a stone statue to be defined as a man. Whether they will actually do so is, however, as likely in the first case as the second. Congress-people are as human as the rest of the population and there is always that element of suspicions against robots."

"Even now?"

"Even now. We would all allow the fact that you have

earned the prize of humanity and yet there would remain the fear of setting an undesirable precedent."

"What precedent? I am the only free robot, the only one of my type, and there will never be another. You may consult U. S. Robots."

" 'Never' is a long time, Andrew—or, if you prefer, Mr. Martin—since I will gladly give you my personal accolade as man. You will find that most Congresspeople will not be willing to set the precedent, no matter how meaningless such a precedent might be. Mr. Martin, you have my sympathy, but I cannot tell you to hope. Indeed—"

She sat back and her forehead wrinkled. "Indeed, if the issue grows too heated, there might well arise a certain sentiment, both inside the Legislature and outside, for that dismantling you mentioned. Doing away with you could turn out to be the easiest way of resolving the dilemma. Consider that before deciding to push matters."

Andrew said, "Will no one remember the technique of prosthetology, something that is almost entirely mine?"

"It may seem cruel, but they won't. Or if they do, it will be remembered against you. It will be said you did it only for yourself. It will be said it was part of a campaign to roboticize human beings, or to humanify robots; and in either case evil and vicious. You have never been part of a political hate campaign, Mr. Martin, and I tell you that you will be the object of vilification of a kind neither you nor I would credit and there would be people who'll believe it all. Mr. Martin, let your life be." She rose and, next to Andrew's seated figure, she seemed small and almost childlike.

Andrew said, "If I decide to fight for my humanity, will you be on my side?"

She thought, then said, "I will be—insofar as I can be. If at any time such a stand would appear to threaten my political future, I may have to abandon you, since it is not an issue I feel to be at the very root of my beliefs. I am trying to be honest with you."

"Thank you, and I will ask no more. I intend to fight this through whatever the consequences, and I will ask you for your help only for as long as you can give it."

19.

It was not a direct fight. Feingold and Martin counseled patience and Andrew muttered grimly that he had an endless supply of that. Feingold and Martin then entered on a campaign to narrow and restrict the area of combat.

They instituted a lawsuit denying the obligation to pay debts to an individual with a prosthetic heart on the grounds that the possession of a robotic organ removed humanity, and with it the constitutional rights of human beings.

They fought the matter skillfully and tenaciously, losing at every step but always in such a way that the decision was forced to be as broad as possible, and then carrying it by way of appeals to the World Court.

It took years, and millions of dollars.

When the final decision was handed down, DeLong held what amounted to a victory celebration over the legal loss. Andrew was, of course, present in the company offices on the occasion.

"We've done two things, Andrew," said DeLong, "both of which are good. First of all, we have established the fact that no number of artifacts in the human body causes it to cease being a human body. Secondly, we have engaged public opinion in the question in such a way as to put it fiercely on the side of a broad interpretation of humanity since there is not a human being in existence who does not hope for prosthetics if that will keep him alive."

"And do you think the Legislature will now grant me my humanity?" asked Andrew.

DeLong looked faintly uncomfortable. "As to that, I cannot be optimistic. There remains the one organ which the World Court has used as the criterion of humanity. Human beings have an organic cellular brain and robots have a platinum-iridium positronic brain if they have one at all—and you certainly have a positronic brain . . . No, Andrew, don't get that look in your eyes. We lack the knowledge to duplicate the work of a cellular brain in artificial structures close enough to the organic type to allow it to fall within the Court's decision. Not even you could do it."

"What ought we do, then?"

"Make the attempt, of course. Congresswoman Li-Hsing will be on our side and a growing number of other Congresspeople. The President will undoubtedly go along with a majority of the Legislature in this matter."

"Do we have a majority?"

"No, far from it. But we might get one if the public will allow its desire for a broad interpretation of humanity to extend to you. A small chance, I admit, but if you do not with to give up, we must gamble for it."

"I do not wish to give up."

20.

Congresswoman Li-Hsing was considerably older than she had been when Andrew had first met her. Her transparent garments were long gone. Her hair was now close-cropped and her coverings were tubular. Yet still Andrew clung, as closely as he could within the limits of reasonable taste, to the style of clothing that had prevailed when he had first adopted clothing over a century before.

She said, "We've gone as far as we can, Andrew. We'll try once more after recess, but, to be honest, defeat is certain and the whole thing will have to be given up. All my most recent efforts have only earned me a certain defeat in the coming congressional campaign."

"I know," said Andrew, "and it distresses me. You said once you would abandon me if it came to that. Why have you not done so?"

"One can change one's mind, you know. Somehow, abandoning you became a higher price than I cared to pay for just one more term. As it is, I've been in the Legislature for over a quarter of a century. It's enough."

"Is there no way we can change minds, Chee?"

"We've changed all that are amenable to reason. The rest—the majority—cannot be moved from their emotional antipathies."

"Emotional antipathy is not a valid reason for voting one way or the other."

"I know that, Andrew, but they don't advance emotional antipathy as their reason."

Andrew said cautiously, "It all comes down to the brain, then, but must we leave it at the level of cells versus positrons? Is there no way of forcing a functional definition. Must we say that a brain is made of this or that? May we not say that a brain is something—anything—capable of a certain level of thought?"

"Won't work," said Li-Hsing. "Your brain is man-made, the human brain is not. Your brain is constructed, theirs developed. To any human being who is intent on keeping up the barrier between himself and a robot, those differences are a steel wall a mile high and a mile thick."

"If we could get at the course of their antipathy—the very source of—"

"After all your years," said Li-Hsing sadly, "you are still trying to reason out the human being. Poor Andrew, don't be angry, but it's the robot in you that drives you in that direction."

"I don't know," said Andrew. "If I could bring myself—"

1. (reprise)

If he could bring himself—

He had known for a long time it might come to that, and in the end he was at the surgeon's. He found one, skillful enough for the job at hand, which meant a robot surgeon, for no human surgeon could be trusted in this connection, either in ability or in intention.

The surgeon could not have performed the operation on a human being, so Andrew, after putting off the moment of decision with a sad line of questioning that reflected the turmoil within himself, put the First Law to one side by saying, "I, too, am a robot."

He then said, as firmly as he had learned to form the words even at human beings over these past decades, "I *order* you to carry through the operation on me."

In the absence of the First Law, an order so firmly given from one who looked so much like a man activated the Second Law sufficiently to carry the day.

21.

Andrew's feeling of weakness was, he was sure, quite imaginary. He had recovered from the operation. Nevertheless, he leaned, as unobtrusively as he could manage, against the wall. It would be entirely too revealing to sit.

Li-Hsing said, "The final vote will come this week,

Andrew. I've been able to delay it no longer, and we must lose . . . And that will be it, Andrew."

Andrew said, "I am grateful for your skill at delay. It gave me the time I needed, and I took the gamble I had to."

"What gamble is this?" asked Li-Hsing with open concern.

"I couldn't tell you, or the people at Feingold and Martin. I was sure I would be stopped. See here, if it is the brain that is at issue, isn't the greatest difference of all the matter of immortality? Who really cares what a brain looks like or is built of or how it was formed? What matters is that brain cells die; *must* die. Even if every other organ in the body is maintained or replaced, the brain cells, which cannot be replaced without changing and therefore killing the personality, must eventually die.

"My own positronic pathways have lasted nearly two centuries without perceptible change and can last for centuries more. Isn't *that* the fundamental barrier? Human beings can tolerate an immortal robot, for it doesn't matter how long a machine lasts. They cannot tolerate an immortal human being, since their own mortality is endurable only so long as it is universal. And for that reason they won't make me a human being."

Li-Hsing said, "What is it you're leading up to, Andrew?"

"I have removed that problem. Decades ago, my positronic brain was connected to organic nerves. Now, one last operation has arranged that connection in such a way that slowly—quite slowly—the potential is being drained from my pathways."

Li-Hsing's finely wrinkled face showed no expression for a moment. Then her lips tightened. "Do you mean you've arranged to die, Andrew? You can't have. That violates the Third Law."

"No," said Andrew, "I have chosen between the death of

my body and the death of my aspirations and desires. To have let my body live at the cost of the greater death is what would have violated the Third Law."

Li-Hsing seized his arm as though she were about to shake him. She stopped herself. "Andrew, it won't work. Change it back."

"It can't be. Too much damage was done. I have a year to live—more or less. I will last through the two hundredth anniversary of my construction. I was weak enough to arrange that."

"How can it be worth it? Andrew, you're a fool."

"If it brings me humanity, that will be worth it. If it doesn't, it will bring an end to striving and that will be worth it, too."

And Li-Hsing did something that astonished herself. Quietly, she began to weep.

22.

It was odd how that last deed caught at the imagination of the world. All that Andrew had done before had not swayed them. But he had finally accepted even death to be human and the sacrifice was too great to be rejected.

The final ceremony was timed, quite deliberately, for the two hundredth anniversary. The World President was to sign the act and make it law and the ceremony would be visible on a global network and would be beamed to the Lunar state and even to the Martian colony.

Andrew was in a wheelchair. He could still walk, but only shakily.

With mankind watching, the World President said, "Fifty years ago, you were declared a Sesquicentennial Robot, Andrew." After a pause, and in a more solemn tone, he said, "Today we declare you a Bicentennial Man, Mr. Martin."

And Andrew, smiling, held out his hand to shake that of the President.

23.

Andrew's thoughts were slowly fading as he lay in bed.

Desperately he seized at them. Man! He was a man! He wanted that to be his last thought. He wanted to dissolve—die—with that.

He opened his eyes one more time and for one last time recognized Li-Hsing waiting solemnly. There were others, but those were only shadows, unrecognizable shadows. Only Li-Hsing stood out against the deepening gray. Slowly, inchingly, he held out his hand to her and very dimly and faintly felt her take it.

She was fading in his eyes, as the last of his thoughts trickled away.

But before she faded completely, one last fugitive thought came to him and rested for a moment on his mind before everything stopped.

"Little Miss," he whispered, too low to be heard.

TRUE LOVE

My name is Joe. That is what my colleague, Milton Davidson, calls me. He is a programmer and I am a computer program. I am part of the Multivac-complex and am connected with other parts all over the world. I know everything. Almost everything.

I am Milton's private program. His Joe. He understands more about programming than anyone in the world, and I am his experimental model. He has made me speak better than any other computer can.

"It is just a matter of matching sounds to symbols, Joe," he told me. "That's the way it works in the human brain even though we still don't know what symbols there are in the brain. I know the symbols in yours, and I can match them to words, one-to-one." So I talk. I don't think I talk as well as I think, but Milton says I talk very well. Milton has never married, though he is nearly forty years old. He has never found the right woman, he told me. One day he said, "I'll find her yet, Joe. I'm going to find the best. I'm going to have true love and you're going to help me. I'm tired of improving you in order to solve the problems of the world. Solve *my* problem. Find me true love."

I said, "What is true love?"

"Never mind. That is abstract. Just find me the ideal girl. You are connected to the Multivac-complex so you can reach the data banks of every human being in the world. We'll eliminate them all by groups and classes until we're left with only one person. The perfect person. She will be for me."

I said, "I am ready."

He said, "Eliminate all men first."

It was easy. His words activated symbols in my molecular valves. I could reach out to make contact with the accumulated data on every human being in the world. At his words, I withdrew from 3,784,982,874 men. I kept contact with 3,786,112,090 women.

He said, "Eliminate all younger than twenty-five; all older than forty. Then eliminate all with an IQ under 120; all with a height under 150 centimeters and over 175 centimeters."

He gave me exact measurements; he eliminated women with living children; he eliminated women with various genetic characteristics. "I'm not sure about eye color," he said. "Let that go for a while. But no red hair. I don't like red hair."

After two weeks, we were down to 235 women. They all spoke English very well. Milton said he didn't want a language problem. Even computer-translation would get in the way at intimate moments.

"I can't interview 235 women," he said. "It would take too much time, and people would discover what I am doing."

"It would make trouble," I said. Milton had arranged me to do things I wasn't designed to do. No one knew about that.

"It's none of their business," he said, and the skin on his

face grew red. "I tell you what, Joe, I will bring in holographs, and you check the list for similarities."

He brought in holographs of women. "These are three beauty contest winners," he said. "Do any of the 235 match?"

Eight were very good matches and Milton said, "Good, you have their data banks. Study requirements and needs in the job market and arrange to have them assigned here. One at a time, of course." He thought a while, moved his shoulders up and down, and said, "Alphabetical order."

That is one of the things I am not designed to do. Shifting people from job to job for personal reasons is called manipulation. I could do it now because Milton had arranged it. I wasn't supposed to do it for anyone but him, though.

The first girl arrived a week later. Milton's face turned red when he saw her. He spoke as though it were hard to do so. They were together a great deal and he paid no attention to me. One time he said, "Let me take you to dinner."

The next day he said to me, "It was no good, somehow. There was something missing. She is a beautiful woman, but I did not feel any touch of true love. Try the next one."

It was the same with all eight. They were much alike. They smiled a great deal and had pleasant voices, but Milton always found it wasn't right. He said, "I can't understand it, Joe. You and I have picked out the eight women who, in all the world, look the best to me. They are ideal. Why don't they please me?"

I said, "Do you please them?"

His eyebrows moved and he pushed one fist hard against his other hand. "That's it, Joe. It's a two-way street. If I am not their ideal, they can't act in such a way as to be my ideal. I must be their true love, too, but how do I do that?" He seemed to be thinking all that day.

The next morning he came to me and said, "I'm going to

leave it to you, Joe. All up to you. You have my data bank, and I am going to tell you everything I know about myself. You fill up my data bank in every possible detail but keep all additions to yourself."

"What will I do with the data bank, then, Milton?"

"Then you will match it to the 235 women. No, 227. Leave out the eight you've seen. Arrange to have each undergo a psychiatric examination. Fill up their data banks and compare them with mine. Find correlations." (Arranging psychiatric examinations is another thing that is against my original instructions.)

For weeks, Milton talked to me. He told me of his parents and his siblings. He told me of his childhood and his schooling and his adolescence. He told me of the young women he had admired from a distance. His data bank grew and he adjusted me to broaden and deepen my symbol-taking.

He said, "You see, Joe, as you get more and more of me in you, I adjust you to match me better and better. You get to think more like me, so you understand me better. If you understand me well enough, then any woman, whose data bank is something you understand as well, would be my true love." He kept talking to me and I came to understand him better and better.

I could make longer sentences and my expressions grew more complicated. My speech began to sound a good deal like his in vocabulary, word order and style.

I said to him one time, "You see, Milton, it isn't a matter of fitting a girl to a physical ideal only. You need a girl who is a personal, emotional, temperamental fit to you. If that happens, looks are secondary. If we can't find the fit in these 227, we'll look elsewhere. We will find someone who won't care how you look either, or how anyone would look, if only there is a personality fit. What are looks?"

"Absolutely," he said. "I would have known this if I had

had more to do with women in my life. Of course, thinking about it makes it all plain now."

We always agreed; we thought so like each other.

"We shouldn't have any trouble, now, Milton, if you'll let me ask you questions. I can see where, in your data bank, there are blank spots and unevennesses."

What followed, Milton said, was the equivalent of a careful psychoanalysis. Of course, I was learning from the psychiatric examinations of the 227 women—on all of which I was keeping close tabs.

Milton seemed quite happy. He said, "Talking to you, Joe, is almost like talking to another self. Our personalities have come to match perfectly."

"So will the personality of the woman we choose."

For I had found her and she was one of the 227 after all. Her name was Charity Jones and she was an Evaluator at the Library of History in Wichita. Her extended data bank fits ours perfectly. All the other women had fallen into discard in one respect or another as the data banks grew fuller, but with Charity there was increasing and astonishing resonance.

I didn't have to describe her to Milton. Milton had coordinated my symbolism so closely with his own I could tell the resonance directly. It fit me.

Next it was a matter of adjusting the work sheets and job requirements in such a way as to get Charity assigned to us. It must be done very delicately, so no one would know that anything illegal had taken place.

Of course, Milton himself knew, since it was he who arranged it and that had to be taken care of too. When they came to arrest him on grounds of malfeasance in office, it was, fortunately, for something that had taken place ten years ago. He had told me about it, of course, so it was easy to arrange—and he won't talk about me for that would make his offense much worse.

He's gone, and tomorrow is February 14. Valentine's Day. Charity will arrive then with her cool hands and her sweet voice. I will teach her how to operate me and how to care for me. What do looks matter when our personalities will resonate?

I will say to her, "I am Joe, and you are my true love."